Also by John Morsell

Death at the End of the Road

In this, the first of the Charlie Skyler mystery series, Charlie and his quirky friends find themselves embroiled in an intrigue involving several murders, an eccentric drug lord, mysterious government agents, and psychopathic assassins. The unique coastal Alaskan town of Homer provides the back drop for their various adventures as they play detective and, at the same time, defend themselves against vengeful members of a widespread drug distribution ring with roots in the Vietnam War.

— Five Star Chanticleer Review —

"A delightful suspense with splashes of humor, and some romance, "Death at the End of the Road" is a book you won't want to miss, especially if you yearn to live vicariously through characters of nontraditional lifestyles and appreciate the natural scenery of one of the most beautiful places in the US."

—CHANTICLEER REVIEWS

The Rare Earth Murders

Charlie Skyler and his quirky friends find themselves embroiled in an intrigue involving bear-ravaged bodies, a corrupt mining company, amoral mercenaries, and treks through the wilderness. The unique coastal Alaskan town of Homer provides the backdrop for their adventures as they play detective and unravel a complex conspiracy to extract minerals for a foreign government.

Project Nemesis

A Charlie Skyler Alaskan Mystery

JOHN MORSELL

Library of Congress Control Number: 2026901461

ISBN: 979-8-218918-29-3 (Paperback)
ISBN: 979-8-218918-30-9 (eBook)

Book design: Melissa Vail Coffman

Printed by Village Books Publishing

Village Books
1200 11th Street
Bellingham, WA 98225

In memory of Ann and Scott

Author's Introduction

The town of Homer on Alaska's Kenai Peninsula and the surrounding Lower Cook Inlet environs are, of course, real places. I have tried to describe the area's geographical, ecological, and historical aspects of the area accurately throughout the book. I assume full responsibility for any inaccuracies that may occur. It should be noted, however, that Project Nemesis is a work of fiction, and, as such, some of the specific locations and circumstances integral to the plot are just plain made up. I apologize to anyone familiar with the area if this juxtaposition of real and unreal causes confusion or consternation.

Cast of Characters

Charlie Skyler: Boat-dwelling ecotour guide whose curiosity often leads to impromptu, if unhealthy, detective work.

Kate Perkins: Swamp-dwelling Midwest transplant who becomes Charlie's partner and gets sucked into Charlie's intrigues.

Johann Sebastian Bachman (JB): Enigmatic retired hippie academic with special skills and a mysterious background.

Beverly Milford: Former DEA agent and current private detective with a bulldog mentality, love of Alaska, and JB's partner.

Bob Stillwater (Super Trooper): Enthusiastic Alaska State Trooper.

Dr. Mort French: Medical Examiner, forensic pathologist.

Stanley Krupp: Political operative with residences in bush Alaska and Washington, D.C.

Richard Vandorn: Harbor murder victim and Senator Strunk's Chief of Staff.

Michael Vandorn: Richard's brother and attorney.

Senator Elmore Strunk: Crude U.S. senator with ambitions to attain greater power.

John Melman: Clueless associate of Stanley Krupp.

Agent Rasmusson: Head of the FBI detail investigating the harbor murder.

Karl: Retired intelligence operative, JB's old boss.

Ralph Neff: Head of the Vice President's security detail.

Dick Whelan: Assassin No. 1. Sniper assigned to eliminate the Vice President.

Gloria Estevez: Homeland Security Secretary.

Ben Madison: Assassin No. 2. Hired by Senator Strunk to kill Gloria Estevez.

Jannis Kaslewsky: Assassin No. 3. Ex son-in-law of Senator Strunk with a criminal streak.

Nate Bacchus: Assassin No. 4. Senator Strunk's fixer with violent tendencies.

George Schuler: Assistant Deputy Director of the FBI.

John Christianson: Director of the FBI.

Randall Howard: Attorney General.

Prologue

Washington, DC. – Three Months Prior to Present Day

A STOUT ELDERLY MAN, DRESSED all in black, slipped into the underground parking garage of a swanky high-rise apartment building in the Georgetown District of Washington, DC. Making his way through the maze of parking spaces, he located a doorway marked "stairwell." Earlier that day, he had followed a young woman on the building's janitorial staff and removed her master access card from her purse while she was waiting at a crowded crosswalk. The stolen card opened the door without a problem.

The stairway was dirty and lit only by individual bulbs hanging from the ceiling. Obviously, the tenants used the elevators exclusively, and little thought was given to stairwell maintenance. It was 3:00 am, and the only sign of life was the faint sound of water running somewhere in the building. The man climbed to the fifth floor and carefully peered around the fire door into the hallway that accessed the entrances to four upscale apartments. He moved to the second apartment on his left and put his ear to the door. There was no sound from within.

The key card opened the door with only a faint click. Holding the door slightly ajar, the man in black listened for about fifteen seconds, then soundlessly entered the main living area. Dim city light from the windows illuminated a large room paneled in dark wood with floor-to-ceiling bookshelves along one wall. The décor was plainly masculine, the dark paneling complemented by a large couch of distressed 'bomber jacket' leather. Matching easy chairs faced the couch with a heavy natural wood coffee table between them. A large wine-colored Persian rug covered most of the living room floor. Picture windows looked out over a park five stories below. This was prime real estate.

A quick reconnaissance indicated a modern kitchen at one end of the living room and a hallway, presumably leading to bedrooms and a bathroom, at the other end. The bedroom door on the left was open, providing a view of a room filled with office equipment. The door on the right was closed, but he could hear someone snoring on the other side.

The man in black knew the next minute was critical to the success of his mission. The fact that the bedroom was in the interior of the apartment with no common walls abutting other apartments was a stroke of luck. Sound would be muffled, and disturbance of the other tenants was unlikely. He slowly opened the door and, in the dim illumination of a night-light, saw that his quarry was indeed in bed, creating a very large lump. Clarence Ayers was an unattractive, obese man with a fleshy face, ruddy complexion, and reddish hair. The man in black approached the side of the bed, aimed a silenced .22 caliber handgun at Ayer's head, and pulled the trigger twice. He immediately left the bedroom and closed the door.

As he retreated through the living room, he saw a folder on the coffee table, which had the appearance of a government document. In the beam of a small flashlight, he could make out an official-looking seal on the cover stamped "TOP SECRET" in large letters. He was extremely curious but did not want to spend any more time than necessary in Ayer's apartment. He listened for noise in the building, but all was quiet. And Ayers obviously was not going anywhere. He decided there was little risk of a short delay. He sat on the couch, opened the folder by unwinding the string closure, and pulled out a bound report of about twenty-five pages. The words "Project Nemesis" were centered on the title page. He read the introduction and quickly paged through the report. The hair stood up on the back of his neck. *Holy shit*, thought the man in black.

He stuck the folder inside his jacket and retraced his steps out of the apartment, down the stairwell, out through the garage, and onto the quiet street.

Chapter 1

Present Day

THE WINDSHIELD WIPERS FRANTICALLY tried to keep up with the deluge as JB's old jeep plowed through the puddles along East End Road. The rhythm of noisy wipers always reminded JB of the lyrics from his favorite folk rock song, "Me and Bobby McGee." He began to sing the song to the beat of the wipers while his partner, Beverly, rolled her eyes and tried to keep from laughing.

JB and Beverly were on their way home from the Rusty Harpoon, a local pub where they had been listening to an excellent Celtic band. The late spring weather in Southcentral Alaska had pretty much sucked for the last week, thereby limiting activities to pub crawling or sitting at home.

The Jeep turned left onto the gravel drive that led uphill to Beverly's cabin. Because of the heavy rain, the quarter-mile-long road was developing a nasty washboard surface as well as some deep puddles and potholes. Avoiding the bumps was impossible, and the Jeep's rigid suspension did not enhance comfort. Finally reaching the cabin, they parked under an attached carport.

JB unfolded his tall, lanky body and stepped down from the vehicle into a puddle. His wild brown hair protruded randomly from under his navy-blue watch cap, contributing to his naturally disheveled appearance. Beverly, on the other hand, always seemed to project a clean-cut aura, apparently without trying. She was of medium height, compact and very fit. Her bright blue eyes, short blond hair, and animated face exemplified cuteness, sometimes catching people off guard. In actuality, she was tough, reinforced by her stint at Quantico, where, in a former life, she had trained to be a DEA agent.

The couple entered through the front door. Beverly had purchased the small, well-made cottage in the town of Homer on Alaska's Kenai Peninsula the year before and coerced JB to abandon his beloved sailboat, the *Otterly Ridiculous*, and move in. JB reluctantly admitted that the cottage was more comfortable than his cramped boat.

One living room table lamp had been left on while they were at the pub. As they entered the room, they were surprised and shocked to see a large elderly man with a squarish face, light complexion, and blonde buzz-cut hair casually holding an automatic handgun facing them on the couch. He wore a yellow fisherman's slicker, jeans, and calf-high rubber boots. A brown, legal-size document folder was on his lap.

"Who the hell are you?" asked the unflappable JB.

"I guess we've never been formally introduced. I'm Aldo," replied the mysterious stranger.

"Holy shit," said Beverly. While neither JB nor Beverly had been in close proximity to Aldo, they both felt like they knew him because of their investigation of Aldo's drug distribution syndicate three years earlier. Aldo had escaped the clutches of the law by fleeing to an unknown location in the Caribbean.

"I'd have thought you'd still be hanging out on the beach. You're taking a big chance coming here," said JB.

"Yeah, well, things change."

"So, what do you want?" asked Beverly as she assessed the situation for possible escape.

"Believe it or not, I'm not here to hassle you guys. In fact, I need your help."

"Aldo, you're a wanted felon. Any help we provide would be seen as aiding and abetting a fugitive," said Beverly.

"I'm well aware of that, which is why I'm holding you at gunpoint. If it ever comes out that I was here, that should give you some deniability, not to mention the fact that you guys are both formidable adversaries, and I probably wouldn't stand much of a chance in a confrontation. But I'm hoping that it doesn't come to that."

"This is crazy. Why don't you explain why you're here?" said JB.

"I sort of accidentally stumbled on a secret document that may be very important and dangerous," said Aldo as he slid the folder across the coffee table toward JB. "This is a copy. I still have the original. The gist of the document is that some unhappy people in the intelligence establishment have developed a plan to get rid of selected persons at the highest levels of government so that guys more favorable to their political interests can take over. The long-term goal seems to be to take over the reins of government. It may seem strange to you that I even care about this stuff, considering that my government wants to put me in jail. Believe it or not, I'm a pretty patriotic guy, and I don't like the idea of a bunch of traitorous black ops whackos taking over control, especially since one of them killed my son."

"I don't suppose you're going to tell us how you happened upon this mysterious document," said Beverly.

"That's probably not a good idea. But I suspect you can figure it out if you give it some thought," replied Aldo.

"So, why come to us?" asked JB.

"The fact that you and your buddies fucked up my business a couple years ago indicates that you're very resourceful and have had experience with government law enforcement agencies. Also, past experience suggests that JB has special knowledge of the shadowy aspects of our government, which might come in handy. And, finally, it looks like Alaska may be the location of the first planned activities, and you guys are already here."

"So, your plan is to just hand this thing over to us so we can save the country," said JB. "That seems like kind of a large and scary responsibility to put it mildly. Wouldn't it work better if you anonymously turned the document over to some government official?"

"Maybe, but what are the chances of anything actually getting done? After you read the document, you'll see that some of the plans are already underway, and Homer may well be an initial focal point." replied Aldo.

"What exactly do you think we're going to be able to do with this information?" asked Beverly.

"Obviously, you need to read it first. You'll see that there are some secret meetings planned near here. Maybe a first step would be to collect intelligence to back up the idea that something dangerous is actually going on. I suspect eventually state and federal authorities will need to be alerted. Still, it looks like at least some in the federal intelligence community and maybe Congress are part of the conspiracy. Also, local law enforcement may be complicit, given the political leanings of some folks around here."

"Jesus, this looks like a total mess. The kind of thing that could screw up our lives completely or maybe get us killed," JB said.

"What you do with this information is totally up to you. I felt I had to give it to somebody. I'm going to disappear again," said Aldo. "I suggest you don't follow me or notify law enforcement. You won't be able to find me. I know my way around this country better than anyone."

Aldo stood while carefully watching the flummoxed couple, pulled up the hood on his slicker, and exited out the back door into the rain and mud, vanishing like a ghost.

"Well, that was interesting," said Beverly after Aldo had disappeared.

"Interesting is a massive understatement," said JB. "I suggest we first find a good place to hide the document. I'm too tired and inebriated to read it now. Let's go to bed and decide what to do in the morning."

"Do you really think you're going to be able to sleep?" added Beverly as she headed for the bedroom.

"I don't know," JB said.

———◆———

The following morning dawned to clear skies and gentle breezes. The puddles from the night before gradually began to dry up. The sun shining on the wet, dark-shingled roof of the cabin caused misty vapor to rise above the roof and disappear into the trees.

Ironically, Beverly had ended up in Homer because of Aldo. She grew up in Los Angeles, the daughter of pretty normal, if boring, parents. She followed the expected upper-middle-class college trajectory, graduating from USC with an accounting degree. Her first job with an accounting firm proved to be mind-numbingly monotonous. Craving more excitement, Beverly applied to the Drug Enforcement Agency and graduated with flying colors from the DEA Training Academy.

She accepted a job with the DEA office in Los Angeles and was assigned, along with her supervisor, to look into a drug operation headquartered in Homer, Alaska. She ended up working with JB and their friends, Charlie and Kate, to dismantle a complicated trafficking syndicate. Somehow, she and JB fell in love—a strait-laced DEA agent connecting with a hippie boat-dweller with a mysterious past. She quit the DEA, moved to Homer, bought a cabin with JB, and started a private detective agency.

Beverly's cabin was pretty basic in layout, consisting of a combination living, dining and kitchen area, two bedrooms, and a large bathroom. But the original owner and builder had been a serious craftsman, and the interior was beautiful. Alaska birch floors, a knotty cedar ceiling, and light-colored walls were anchored by an intricate stone fireplace. The floor-to-ceiling masonry consisted of several rock types with various nooks built into the structure filled with curios from the couple's travels.

When Beverly awoke at seven o'clock, the space in the bed beside her was empty. She wandered into the living room in her flannel nightgown (Alaska nights are cold) and found JB in his favorite easy chair, reading the disturbing document obtained from Aldo. She grabbed a cup of coffee from the kitchen and sat next to him. "So, what do you think?"

"All I can say is, wow," answered JB. "You should probably read it before we discuss where the heck we go from here."

"Do you have any theories on where Aldo found it?"

"It seems like there's only one possibility, which I suspect you've already thought of."

"Yeah, Ayer's apartment in Washington."

Clarence Ayers was a shadowy intelligence operative whom they had unfortunately encountered several years earlier. Beverly and JB had worked with their friends Charlie and Kate to help break up a drug distribution syndicate led by none other than Aldo Fenstrom. Aldo's psychotic son, Robert, was captured by JB and then shot by an unknown assailant. Robert had been trained as an assassin for Ayers' secret intelligence group, but left government service and ended up as a sort of enforcer in Aldo's organization. As Robert's former boss, Ayers did not want Robert talking to law enforcement about the questionable activities of his top-secret group. It was strongly suspected that Ayers ordered the assassination of Robert Fenstrom.

Several months earlier, Ayers had been found dead in his apartment. The official cause of death was a heart attack; however, rumors in the Washington D.C. law enforcement community suggested that his death might not have been entirely natural. It was known that Aldo was very upset by the murder of his son and vowed vengeance. JB's old boss in Washington, D.C., speculated that Aldo had killed Ayers.

"I wonder how that worked. Was the document just sitting out in the open in Ayers' apartment, and Aldo just happened to look at it?" JB said.

"I guess it doesn't matter now. Unfortunately, we've got it. So, what does it say?"

"I'm not all the way through it yet, but it seems to be a combination manifesto and detailed planning document for the initial stages of a plot to assume enough power in Congress and the executive branch to call the shots.

"That's crazy. Exactly how do they plan to accomplish a takeover?"

"That's not real clear from what I've read so far. The implication is that they plan to selectively substitute persons loyal to their cause into key positions. It sounds like they're not going to depend on elections to achieve their goals."

"That sounds ominous. What do you think we should do? On the one hand, a fugitive wanted for murder was in our house last night, and we may be obligated to report the contact. On the other hand, reporting the contact would open the whole thing up to public scrutiny and possibly prevent attempts to quietly quash whatever is going on."

"I think we should both carefully read through the document, then talk with Charlie and Kate."

"Do we really want to get them involved in our illegal acts?"

"I think we need their brain power. Plus, you and Kate are supposed to be partners, and it would be pretty hard to keep a secret this big. I think this dilemma requires the full force of the four Mooseketeers."

Chapter 2

The cabin of Charlie's boat, the *Shearwater*, was crowded on Saturday morning. Charlie, Kate, JB, and Beverly sat around the galley table. Each had coffee. A plate of pastries occupied the center of the table. Buster, the black cat, lay fluidly on the counter next to the Bristol oil stove, resembling a feline Rorschach test. The spring rain had finally stopped, and sunshine flooded the pilothouse windows, warming the small space. The glaciers across the bay sparkled in the bright light, contrasting with the dark green of the forest and the blue of the bay in the foreground.

The four friends had been thrown together several years earlier as inconveniently located dead bodies thrust them into a world of drug-fueled conspiracy and impromptu detective work. But their individual histories were unique, each having ended up in Homer for different reasons. One common element was the fact that Homer is literally the end of the line. The many restless travelers entering Homer for the first time were faced with a couple of choices—they could turn around and retrace their steps to wherever they came from, returning to lives that they had rejected, or they could start a new life in the "hamlet by the sea"—so named by Brother Isaiah, the sole refugee from one of several defunct hippie communes established in Homer in the 1960s.

Charlie Skyler was the first to arrive in Homer as a young man in the late 1990s, searching for a location where he could settle down and earn a living as a commercial fisherman. He liked the small town at the end of the road because of its beauty, eccentric occupants, and fishery potential. The fact that his old Chevy pickup died just as he arrived in town contributed to his decision to stay.

Using money earned by crewing on various commercial fishing boats, Charlie bought an old forty-foot purse seine boat and tried his hand at salmon fishing. Long nets stored on the large back deck were used to encircle schools of salmon. When the school was trapped within the circle, the bottom of the net was "pursed" like the end of a stuff sack, creating a bag of squirming fish. The net was pulled aboard using a large hydraulic block, and the fish were dumped into a hold in the middle of the deck. The galley cabin, pilot house, and crew quarters were as far forward as possible to allow space for the large deck.

Unfortunately, dwindling fish resources and collapsing fish markets caused Charlie to change direction. He converted his boat to make it suitable for wildlife tours and modified the Shearwater to provide comfortable live-aboard accommodations. The large fish hold was converted to an owner's cabin with a queen bed and small bathroom. Charlie was an accomplished carpenter, and the teak woodwork was carefully crafted to fit the curving lines of the boat hull. Over the years he had shamelessly cultivated an "Alaskan character" persona, enhancing his tourism business.

Charlie was a large man with broad shoulders, a little over six feet tall. His purposefully unkempt blonde hair, full blonde beard, and bright blue eyes provided a sort of Viking aura. Although attractive to the opposite sex, his desire to avoid commitment resulted in numerous failed relationships. He met his current partner, Kate Perkins, as a result of the aforementioned dead bodies—one floating next to his boat and another on the trail to Kate's cabin in the woods—leading to the dramatic events associated with Aldo Fenstrom's drug syndicate.

Kate's spirit and unusual beauty overcame Charlie's desire to remain uncommitted. Her lithe figure, long brown hair, and amazing green eyes sucked him into her soul. Her exotic face combined features of Irish and Eastern European ancestry. Kate had ended up in Homer sort of accidentally after running from a disappointing experience in New York City. Her dream of becoming a dancer was dashed when she flunked several auditions.

To make matters worse, her latest boyfriend had been abusive. She threw her belongings into her compact car and fled the mean city. Without knowing how she got there, Kate somehow arrived at the end of the road in Homer. Later, she realized that she had undergone some sort of mental breakdown.

Although the coastal Alaska environment was totally different from what she had been used to—both ecologically and culturally—she liked the unusual coastal town. She bought a cabin in the woods using money inherited from her grandmother and learned the skills required for an off-the-grid existence. She and Charlie split their time between Charlie's boat and her cabin. Kate had a pretty good job as an administrative manager for FlashFrozen Seafood. Recently, she began learning advanced computer skills and gained expertise as a hacker with the help of her hacker brother in Michigan. She was moonlighting as an investigator for Beverly's private detective firm, Otterly Ridiculous Investigations.

"So, what's so urgent that we had to get up on a Saturday morning?" asked Charlie as JB shoveled a pastry into his mouth.

"We had a very surprising visitor last night," replied Beverly. "Aldo stopped by for a little chat."

"You're kidding!" said Kate. "You guys are still alive, so I guess he didn't shoot you."

"Amazingly, he was friendly," said JB through a mouthful of pastry. "The weird thing is, he wanted our help." JB and Beverly related the events of the previous night and suggested that Charlie and Kate read the mystery document.

"Can you summarize the report so we have some idea what we are dealing with?" asked Charlie.

"The first few pages are a sort of manifesto that describes the desire by this whacko group to take control of the government by selectively eliminating key personnel and replacing them with persons that are sympathetic to their views," said JB. "The remainder consists of more detailed plans for what is apparently the first phase of their plan. Specifically, they seem to be planning to assassinate the vice president during his upcoming visit to Alaska."

"Wow," said Charlie. "And the four of us are supposed to save the world by thwarting this conspiracy?"

"That's about it," replied Beverly.

"That seems like a ridiculously massive responsibility," said Kate. "What's wrong with normal law enforcement?"

"There may be a couple of problems with relying on local or national agencies," said JB as he refilled his coffee mug. "When you read the report, it becomes obvious that persons in the federal intelligence community are involved, and we don't know how deep the involvement goes. Also, it seems like one of the reasons the Kenai Peninsula is an initial focal point for the organizers is the presence of numerous local nutjobs willing to participate. Obviously, the feds are going to need to be notified at some point, but we may need to be careful who we talk to. I'll talk to my contact in D.C. to get his read on which agencies would be best to avoid."

"Unfortunately, the persons involved in the conspiracy are referenced only by number, so we don't know anybody's name," continued JB. "Plus, most of the report is too vague to tell us much about their plans. I don't even know where to start an investigation."

"The document does mention that there will be a meeting of the group at some secret location in Alaska in a couple of weeks," contributed Beverly, "It would obviously be helpful if we could listen in on that meeting. All we have to do is figure out where the meeting is being held."

"Swell! How are we going to do that?" asked Kate.

"I think you guys should read through the document before we do anything else," said JB as he reached for his third pastry. "Since tomorrow is Sunday, let's get together again in the morning and try to think of a way forward."

Chapter 3

Stanley Krupp sat at the small desk in his log cabin in the remote Caribou Hills on a high plateau about forty miles northeast of Homer. The remote cabin perched on the shore of a small lake, surrounded by white spruce and patches of muskeg, with a view of the low mountains to the east. During most of the year, the cabin could only be reached by small plane. A short grassy landing strip had been created by more or less leveling an adjacent meadow. A shiny red Cessna 180 bush plane with fat tundra tires was parked at one end of the airstrip. Off the edge of the strip sat a rusty bulldozer and two large sleds.

The cabin had been hand-constructed by Stanley himself, using spruce logs from the site. Other building materials and essential items needed for remote living had been transported to the area cross-country by tractor-pulled sleds during the winter when the ground and wet muskeg areas were solidly frozen. Although not so common in the twenty-first century, these so-called cat trains were historically used in Alaska to get stuff from place to place. Wet conditions often prevented overland travel during the thawed season. In short, the cabin was nearly impossible to access unless you were brave enough to land a plane on the sketchy airstrip. People living such an existence in Alaska were often unfriendly to unexpected visitors, further discouraging intruders and adding to the cabin's de facto isolation.

The primitive dwelling consisted of one large room plus a bedroom alcove and bath, sort of an efficiency apartment in the wilderness. But inside, it was cozy and well-furnished. A sophisticated diesel generator in an outside shed, combined with battery backup, provided reliable power during cabin occupation. A prominent satellite dish adorning the shake roof seemed discordant with the rest of the setting, but allowed the occupant to communicate with the rest of the world if he so desired.

Stanley was a large, somewhat overweight man with a full black beard and unkempt, thinning black hair tinged with white. His burgeoning middle-aged gut disguised the fact that he was fit and strong. Despite his appearance, Stanley was not your average Alaskan sourdough hermit. He had an undergraduate degree from Harvard and a law degree from Yale, plus three years in the Army Rangers. He was well-connected with numerous important people, mostly located in Washington, D.C. In fact, he spent part of the year in Washington schmoozing with carefully selected politicians and lobbyists.

He was currently tapping away on his laptop, sending encrypted messages via satellite internet. It concerned him greatly that, although they had carefully delivered twenty copies of the secret planning document directly to the participants in the conspiracy, one was now missing. This was a serious development and could potentially scuttle their well-thought-out plans.

Stanley knew that Ayers had died only two days after receiving his copy, and somehow his copy had disappeared. One of the group members broke into Ayers' apartment the day after his death and completed a very thorough search. There had been no sign of the document, but there had been disturbing signs that Ayers' death was not accidental, despite what the official announcement had proclaimed. Stanley's experienced agent noted that the bed had apparently been remade with clean sheets after the removal of the body, but he found some traces of blood on the headboard behind the mattress. It looked like some of Ayers' black ops associates had cleaned the crime scene and whitewashed the true nature of the crime.

If Ayers was murdered, then whoever killed him might have taken the document. Questions remained about whether someone intentionally killed Ayers to obtain the report. If that was the case, then who? And how would they know he had it since no one outside the group knew of its existence? Was there a leak in the group? Did Ayers destroy it for some reason? Did the crime scene cleaners take it? If so, where was it now? Stanley explained all this in a series of secure emails to the other members of his outlaw group.

An additional item of business concerned the proposed group meeting in Alaska scheduled to occur in two weeks. It was agreed that the meeting should proceed as planned. Each member "independently" planned fishing trips to the famous angling waters of the Kenai Peninsula. The fishing excursions would, of course, actually occur and provide cover, not to mention entertainment, for the members of the macho group. Arrangements were made for Stanley to shuttle the men from a private airstrip near Kenai to his hideaway—after their fishing adventures were completed, of course. Flight plans would likely not be filed.

Chapter 4

The strange name, *Wonky*, was artistically scrolled on the stern of the luxurious motor yacht. Inside, blood pooled on the polished teak-and-holly plank floor. A deceased male was draped awkwardly, head downward, on the stairs between the elevated pilot house and the main cabin. Standing beside the body was Alaska State Trooper Bob Stillwater. Dr. Mort French, medical examiner for the Kenai Borough, leaned over the crumpled human form.

Bob thought Dr. Mort looked like a comic book representation of someone who specialized in examining dead bodies—he was tall and thin with a sunken, cadaverous, pale face, small dark eyes, and thinning, wispy brown hair. In contrast to the medical examiner, Bob was a large, stout man built like an old- growth tree stump. Incongruously, he had a roundish pink baby face and buzz-cut hair. His utility belt with assorted weapons and pockets looked like it weighed sixty pounds. Both men were looking at the two bullet holes in the dead man's head. The larger exit wounds had removed several inches of the man's forehead, suggesting a shot from behind. Blood dripping from the head wounds had coagulated on the last two steps like tiny red waterfalls frozen in place.

"So, who is this guy?" asked Bob.

"The ID in his wallet says he's Richard Vandorn, from Washington state," replied Mort as he handed an evidence bag with the wallet to

Bob. "Money and credit cards weren't taken, so theft was probably not a motive."

"How long's he been dead?"

"Probably not more than a couple of hours. A diesel mechanic found him at about eight o'clock. The mechanic was scheduled to do engine maintenance this morning. We're lucky he was discovered so quickly."

"It probably doesn't matter too much to Mr. Vandorn," said the frustrated trooper. "I was going to go fishing today, but I guess my plans have changed."

Bob began looking around the boat. A drawer across from the galley contained vessel registration and Coast Guard documentation. "The boat's a forty-three-foot Nordhavn and is, indeed, registered to Mr. Vandorn. Its home port seems to be San Juan, Washington, so I guess we can conclude that our victim piloted the boat from there to here. That's a pretty long trip for a forty-three-foot boat."

Mort, who considered himself an expert on boats, replied, "We can probably assume that Richard Vandorn was a reasonably skilled mariner. Nordhavns are designed to cross oceans, so they're a cut above the average recreational yacht. Their million-dollar cost not only assures luxury but also seaworthiness and reliability."

Bob began to search the beautiful, teak-lined owner's cabin located amidships below the galley. The stateroom was accessed by a curved stairway, all lined in teak. This boat was way nicer than his house. One of the built-in drawers in a side table adjacent to the queen-sized bed contained a passport in Vandorn's name as well as a badge on a lanyard that permitted entry into the Capitol Building in Washington, D.C. The badge indicated that Vandorn was Chief of Staff for Senator Elmore Strunk. Holy crap, thought Bob. What the hell was he doing in Homer? And why come by boat? I'm going to have to contact the FBI, and the shit is probably about to hit the fan.

Back in the main cabin, Dr. Mort was finishing up. His assistants had bagged and removed the body and collected fingerprints from around the boat. A nine mm bullet was found embedded in the frame of the door that led outside from the cabin to the cockpit.

As Bob came up the stairs from below, Mort said, "It looks like Mr. Vandorn was shot from the pilot house as he was descending the companionway stairs, based on the wound characteristics and the location of the bullet embedded in the cabin door frame. That would also explain the head-downward position on the stairs. It might mean the killer was already aboard when Vandorn arrived, or maybe was a guest on the boat."

No other obvious forensic evidence was found. The killer had likely picked up any shell casings and was apparently careful not to disturb anything.

After Mort and his forensic entourage departed with the body *en route* to the morgue in Kenai, Bob wrapped crime scene tape around the boat and checked for the presence of any potential witnesses on neighboring boats. But all were vacant. Although it was Saturday, the poor weather was not conducive to boating, and most boat owners were snug in their houses.

He then walked to the Harbor Master's office and asked about the visitor on the Nordhavn. The Harbor Master indicated that the yacht had arrived two days prior, and Mr. Vandorn had paid for a week's moorage in advance. Other than that, he had no information on the mysterious visitor. As part of his job, the Harbor Master made obser-vations of the harbor every hour or so, but he had not seen anyone other than Vandorn coming and going to the boat.

Next, Bob walked down the dock to Charlie Skyler's boat, the *Shearwater*. Charlie, Kate, JB, and Beverly were drinking coffee in the galley, and Bob was invited to join them. JB quickly hid the mystery document when he saw Bob approaching.

"So, what's up?" asked JB.

"It looks like another homicidal shit storm is about to hit Homer," replied Bob. The trooper summarized the morning's events for the four friends. "I'm telling you all this, even though I shouldn't, because the FBI will probably get involved. You guys have worked with the troopers on past investigations, and I want to have a third party aware of the situation. My past experience with the FBI suggests that they are going to take over. Some FBI agents tend to be critical of local law enforcement and push them out of the way. I figured you guys are going to get involved somehow anyway. Also, you can provide eyes and ears in the harbor, which could be useful."

Bob thought, *Who am I kidding? Charlie, Kate, JB, and Beverly were instrumental in bringing down Aldo's drug syndicate, as well as a corrupt mining operation involved in two murders last year. I need their help.*

Bob left the harbor and went back to his office. His first call was to his boss in Anchorage. Captain Ross expressed irritation that his Saturday baseball game was being interrupted and was somewhat speechless after hearing the details. He agreed that the FBI needed to be notified because a high-ranking federal government employee was involved. After getting the relevant information from Bob, he called the Special Agent-in-Charge of the Anchorage office at home and informed him about what had happened. The agent was skeptical of the facts and pissed that the murder had occurred on a Saturday, but he reluctantly agreed to notify all the appropriate people.

———◆———

"So, what are the odds that the harbor murder is somehow related to Project Nemesis?" asked Charlie as he reached for another pastry.

"I don't think we have enough information to draw any conclusions. But it's certainly something to think about. Things seem to be getting weirder and weirder," replied Beverly.

"If I recall correctly, Senator Strunk is an extremist from Louisiana with white nationalist tendencies. Maybe he is one of the Nemesis players," suggested JB.

"Let's not get ahead of ourselves," said Charlie. "The national media are bound to get hold of this soon. Investigative reporters may fill in some of the gaps. Meanwhile, we should try to keep a low pro-file, especially with the FBI getting involved."

"I guess this gives me another reason to get in touch with my Washington, D.C. contact. I'm sure he'll be very interested," contrib-uted JB.

"What if your old boss is part of the Project Nemesis conspiracy?" asked Beverly.

"I'd be pretty surprised," answered JB. "But he may have some ideas as to who's involved. The black ops community is full of crazy people. In fact, that's sort of a prerequisite."

"At least we have some names to deal with now," said Kate. "I'll see what I can find out about Richard Vandorn and Senator Strunk."

CHAPTER 5

A LITTLE LATER IN THE afternoon, Kate sent Charlie away, settled in to a comfortable spot at the galley table, booted up her computer, and started to do her thing. Kate was an experienced computer user, but in the last couple of years she had honed her hacking skills and become much more proficient at finding information—sometimes in ways that were less than fully legal. She was tutored by her brother in Michigan, who had been a serious hacker in high school and college but was now working in the legitimate IT industry.

It was obvious that Senator Strunk would have a large internet and social media presence by virtue of his job. So, Kate started her search with Richard Vandorn, hoping his information would be more straightforward. Vandorn grew up in Washington State, received a master's degree in political science from Yale, and started his career as a political groupie by working as a senate page. He worked on the staff of various congressmen and senators until becoming Chief of Staff for Senator Strunk. His permanent residence was San Juan Island in Puget Sound. He lived there with his wife and two teenage children, commuting to Washington, D.C. when needed by the Senator.

It turned out that Vandorn was a pretty boring guy. Social media and internet postings were normal for an active professional in the political sphere. A deep dive on the dark web revealed no unsavory activity. As far as Kate could tell, Vandorn was a boy scout. His personal email and Facebook accounts contained no political exchanges, suggesting that he was careful to separate his government work and personal life. He worked diligently with Senator Strunk to write speeches and draft legislation. He seemed to stay out of trouble and avoid controversy. A brief announcement on two social media sites indicated that Vandorn was taking a two-week vacation while the Senate was in recess.

As might be expected, Vandorn was an avid boater with extensive experience, including an ocean crossing to Hawaii in his Nordhavn. Many photos of the Hawaii trip appeared on Facebook, but, strangely, there were no entries on social media or anywhere else that mentioned a planned boat trip to Homer, Alaska. It seemed odd that Vandorn would not brag about an interesting trip to Alaska, given his previous presence on social media. Kate wished she could look at Vandorn's phone, but, apparently, no phone was found at the crime scene. All in all, Richard Vandorn seemed like an upstanding citizen with no obvious hidden agenda. So, what was he doing in Homer?

Switching gears, Kate began to look into Senator Strunk's life. The amount of information on social media was overwhelming. The main problem was deciding what information was actually significant. As Kate sorted through the political bullshit, it became apparent that Senator Strunk was a polarizing figure with views that did not really fit into any lane. Apparently, he started his career as a CIA analyst, then, strangely, there were no records for a five-year time period. After that, he reappeared in the political limelight big time. Kate thought his life trajectory was similar to JB's, suggesting some kind of secret intelligence work or maybe black ops.

His various public statements on Twitter and elsewhere often seemed angry. He was cynical and suspicious of everything governmental and, consequently, was opposed to most government actions. All of which begged the question in Kate's eyes—why bother to be a senator if you do not want the government to do anything?

"So, what did you find out?" asked Charlie when he returned from running errands in town.

"Vandorn's profile is pretty much what you would expect from a well-educated political insider. There was no indication of any political dirty tricks. The senator, on the other hand, is a very controversial, strident, and obnoxious person. He is deeply suspicious of government and the political process. While we have no good reason to think that Vandorn's murder is connected to the mystery document, Senator Strunk's profile could suggest the possibility."

"But how could a long-distance boat trip by his chief of staff fit into the whole thing?" asked Charlie as he pulled a microbrew from the little fridge under the galley counter.

"I don't know. It doesn't make much sense. Maybe he was simply vacationing," replied Kate.

MEANWHILE, BOB STILLWATER—KNOWN BY some as the Super Trooper because of his zeal in busting formerly illegal marijuana grow operations—sat at his ratty gray, army surplus desk and contemplated his current predicament. It looked like his quiet community was about to be thrust into the national news once again. Life would be much simpler if he did not have to share law enforcement duties with overly macho, uptight federal officials. He sighed, leaned back in his worn desk chair, and stared at the photo of a bikini-clad blond woman cuddling a chainsaw. The wall calendar from a Swedish chainsaw manufacturer had been left there by the previous occupants and was six years out of date. Nevertheless, Bob found it relaxing and had never bothered to remove it.

He had been tasked with making lodging and office arrangements for four FBI agents arriving in Homer on the evening plane from Anchorage. His boss had volunteered his help in finding accommodations, even though the FBI had a whole department whose sole job was logistics. Additionally, it was Bob's unpleasant duty to notify Richard Vandorn's next of kin. After spending a ridiculous amount of time on the telephone, he discovered that Vandorn's only close relative was a brother in Seattle, Michael Vandorn. A Google search indicated that Michael Vandorn was a lawyer and an Assistant Federal Prosecutor. Bob's conversation with Michael had not gone well—as if Bob was somehow responsible for his brother's untimely demise. Michael would also be arriving on the evening plane to make arrangements to transport the body. He requested that Bob meet him at the airport and brief him on the details of the murder. The next couple of days were going to be interesting. *Oh boy*! Bob thought.

Chapter 6

The following morning, a Sunday, Charlie, Kate, JB, and Beverly gathered on the small front porch of Kate's rustic log cabin. The well-built cabin was roughly ten miles northwest of Homer and only accessible via a quarter-mile trail from the roadway. The cabin sat on a small knoll at the edge of a black spruce bog. The tight-fitting logs were a tribute to the skills of the unknown original builder and helped ensure minimal rodent invasion. The heavy door and barred windows discouraged bears from breaking in. The interior featured early fur trapper décor, complete with a wood stove fashioned from a fifty-five-gallon drum and a table made from hand-hewn planks. After moving in three years previously, Kate added colorful pillows, oriental rugs, and various art objects, resulting in an unexpected, cozy, feminine vibe. The Mooseketeers met at the cabin partly because they wanted a quiet, secluded place to discuss strategy for their investigation of Project Nemesis and partly because Kate needed to make sure that the cabin remained undisturbed in her absence.

It was a warm, sunny morning with a light breeze that rustled the aspen leaves and caused the sweet smells of the bog to waft in the direction of the unlikely quartet of snoopy humans. Buster the cat prowled at the edge of the clearing, pretending to be a fierce predator, glad to be sprung from the confines of Charlie's boat. The only thing disturbing the tranquility of the moment was the abundance of annoying insects, specifically mosquitoes and small biting flies locally called 'white sox' because of the white coloration on their ankles, if flies actually had ankles.

"So, have you guys figured out how we're going to save the world?" asked Kate as she passed out mugs of coffee and set a plate of cinnamon rolls between them. "I hope you realize that we are once again putting ourselves in the crosshairs of potentially dangerous people, not to mention violating laws regulating top-secret information."

"I'm working on it," said Charlie as he slapped a mosquito and passed the bug spray.

"Great. I'm anxious to hear what you've come up with, especially since we have no clue where to start looking," quipped Beverly as she slathered bug dope on her arms.

"I may have at least one possibility," said Charlie. "I just got a text from Trooper Bob. Richard Vandorn's brother and only living relative is arriving this evening. Bob will be busy with a herd of FBI agents arriving on the same plane, and he asked me to show Michael Vandorn around. Right now, we have no idea whether Vandorn's murder is connected to Project Nemesis, but it sure seems like a possibility. It seems that Michael is a federal prosecutor, and he may want to get involved in the investigation. Plus, he may have some idea why his brother decided to go on a long boat trip to Alaska without telling anybody. I can try to develop some kind of rapport with him, and hopefully we can eventually trade notes."

"I'll see what I can find out about Michael Vandorn online," added Kate. "And maybe check out some of Homer's more notorious whackos who might be associated with this crazy scheme—maybe rank them according to likely participation."

JB picked up a roll, glanced at all the tiny flies trapped in the frosting, then shrugged his shoulders and ate it in two bites. "That all sounds good. Meanwhile, I can check with my source in Washington, D.C. to see if he has any insight into the conspiracy. Also, one item that was specifically mentioned in the mystery document is the plan to assassinate Vice President Taylor while on a fishing trip, probably on the Kenai River. I can look at maps and try to figure out some likely scenarios—places where a sniper might get a shot and, at the same time, be able to elude the Secret Service. I'm guessing that helicopters or drones might be involved in Secret Service surveillance, so the sniper nest would need to be well hidden with a feasible escape route. All of this is complicated by the fact that the V.P.'s plans will likely be kept secret from the public until the last minute."

"I guess, since all of you guys are giving yourselves assignments," Beverly chimed in. "I could see if I can convince my former analyst at the DEA to do an information dive into some of these characters." Beverly's former colleague, Tammy, had been an outlaw hacker in high school and college. She had been arrested during a protest against a nuclear power plant and made a deal with the DEA to provide cyber security services as part of a community service sentence. The work had evolved into a legitimate full-time IT position with the DEA. But Tammy missed the excitement of hacking on the fringe of legality. Her skills, combined with the resources available to the DEA, could be valuable.

———◆———

"WHAT THE FUCK!" STANLEY Krupp's words echoed within the empty cabin. He was trolling various media sites and came upon the news that Senator Strunk's Chief of Staff, Richard Vandorn, had been murdered in Homer, Alaska. Because of the senator's notoriety, the story had become national news, and the media was salivating with glee at the potential scandal. Stanley had no clue why Richard Vandorn had been in Homer and had a bad feeling there were things going on of which he was unaware. The senator was a member of the Project Nemesis conspiracy, but, as far as he knew, Vandorn was not privy to their secret machinations.

Nevertheless, Vandorn's presence in Homer out of the blue certainly suggested that it could not be a coincidence. Was Strunk aware that his chief of staff was heading to Homer? And why a long boat trip instead of a five-hour plane ride?

He immediately fired off an encrypted email to all members of the group, asking if anybody had any idea what was going on.

Chapter 7

THE SMALL ARRIVAL AREA of the Homer International Airport was crowded as people waited for the evening flight from Anchorage. Charlie and Trooper Bob stood off to the side where they could see out of the window. They observed with amusement the passengers disgorging onto the tarmac. An unusual number wore navy blue suits and aviator sunglasses, immediately identifying them as federal agents. It would be an understatement to say that they stood out from normal casual Alaskans, most of whom were dressed in dirty jeans and rubber boots.

"Which one do you think is Michael Vandorn?" asked Charlie.

"I'm betting on the guy in the chinos and button-down shirt. He looks like a lawyer," said Bob.

"Do the feds know Vandorn is arriving on the same plane?"

"Not that I know of."

"It might be good if we can keep things separated," suggested Charlie. "I'll try to pull Vandorn aside to avoid complications."

"Roger that."

The four federal agents zeroed in on Bob's uniform and introduced themselves to him. Meanwhile, Charlie met Vandorn at the door, introduced himself, helped him retrieve his luggage, and offered to give him a ride to the hotel or anywhere else he wanted to go. Vandorn was tall and exceptionally handsome, resembling Robert

Redford. He moved with athletic grace and confidence. Charlie was thinking that he would be a formidable legal adversary. But right now, he was a grieving brother.

"So, what's your stake in all this?" asked Vandorn as Charlie grabbed his suitcase.

"I guess I don't really have a stake, other than being terminally nosy," replied Charlie. "My friends and I have helped the troopers with a couple of investigations, and I think Bob trusts us. He is concerned that the feds will push him out of the way. He may see us as allies."

"He's probably right about that. As a federal prosecutor, I'm usually on the side of the FBI, but I fear there's more going on here than meets the eye. Is there some place we can talk in private?"

"We can go to my boat. I'll even buy you a beer."

"Sounds good. Maybe I can check into the hotel on the way."

Twenty minutes later, they were walking down the ramp to the harbor at the end of the Homer spit, a six-mile peninsula extending into the middle of Kachemak Bay. Charlie introduced Michael Vandorn to Kate, who was sitting in her normal spot at the galley table of the *Shearwater*, eating potato chips and drinking beer. Kate closed her laptop so Vandorn would not see what she was doing.

"What do you know about my brother's murder?" asked Michael as Charlie handed him a craft beer from a local brewery. "You can be frank. I've dealt with murder before."

"OK. My understanding is he was shot twice in the head by someone inside the boat in the early morning hours," replied Charlie. "His body was discovered a few hours later by a mechanic that your brother contacted for engine work. The body was lying head down on the stairs from the pilot house to the salon, suggesting that the shooter had been in the pilot house when the gun was fired. It's likely a silencer was used since no one nearby heard the shots. A nine mm bullet was found in the door frame leading outside from the salon. No other obvious forensic evidence was found. And no paperwork or documents were found other than boat ownership stuff."

"We're very sorry for your loss," said Kate as she observed Michael's pained expression. "Do you have any idea why Richard decided to drive his boat to Homer?"

"All I know is he was disturbed by something going on with the Senator. Richard was ambitious and politically savvy, but at the same time, he had a strong moral compass. It's not hard to imagine him getting caught in unsavory stuff and not knowing how to get out of it."

"What do you know about Senator Strunk?" asked Kate.

"I only met him once, and my conclusion was that he is a total asshole."

"I guess that sort of sums it up," Charlie remarked. "Something just occurred to me. Assuming that Richard came up here for some reason other than pure recreation, it seems likely that the crime scene people would have found some indication of the reason. I know that some custom yachts have secret compartments built in during the manufacturing process so that owners can hide stuff like guns from border authorities. Do you know if the Nordhavn has a secret compartment?"

"I don't know, but I can probably find out from the manufacturer or dealer," Michael suggested. "I'll call first thing in the morning. Richard had a living trust that included the boat. Since I'm both the heir and executor of the trust, I should be able to assume full possession as soon as the feds are through with it. Richard was unmarried and had no children, and both our parents are dead, so I'm it."

"How about you, Michael?" asked Kate. "You married?"

"No, I'm divorced and happily single. No children to worry about."

"So, you suggested you had suspicions of unsavory stuff going on. Do you have any ideas what that might be?" said Charlie.

"I hadn't really thought much about it until I learned that Richard took a secret boat trip to Alaska and, tragically, isn't going to return. As I think back about the last couple of conversations I had with Richard, it seems obvious that something serious was bothering him. He seemed frightened. When I asked for details, he dodged the question. He was always careful to honor his obligation to the senator not to release information without permission. I just don't know what was going on, but Alaska must play a part somehow."

Michael's mobile phone rang. After stepping out on deck to answer, he spoke for a few minutes, then returned to the galley.

"That was the FBI. They want to meet with me in half an hour at the trooper office. They asked me where I was, and I told them I was in my hotel room. For some reason, even though I'm the only surviving relative, they are treating me like a hostile witness. There doesn't seem to be a lot of compassion going on. They clearly don't want me talking to anyone else. I think the fact that I'm a federal prosecutor with the ability to investigate stuff worries them. This situation just gets weirder and weirder."

"The state trooper, Bob Stillwater, is a nice guy, and I'm sure he will do his best to be understanding," added Charlie. "But maybe our conversations should be kept confidential for now. It would be interesting to see if your movements are monitored, so maybe keep an eye out for a tail."

"Yeah. I was thinking the same thing," replied Michael.

"Would you be willing to get together again after you meet with the feds?" asked Kate. "We'd like to include our friends JB and Beverly. JB has connections with the intelligence community, and Beverly is a former DEA agent currently working as a private detective. I guess we would have to meet secretly."

"OK. Let me see what happens at this meeting. Maybe you can give me your phone numbers."

———— ◆ ————

MICHAEL VANDORN ENTERED THE trooper office and followed voices to the small conference room, which was crowded with men in blue suits, along with Trooper Bob. Bulging armpits indicated the presence of firearms. Voices were raised and conversation was animated. All went quiet as soon as Michael approached the doorway.

As Michael walked in and sat on the only available chair, a stout man with a shaved head at the head of the table stood and introduced himself as Agent Rasmussen. He did not bother to introduce the other three agents.

"Mr. Vandorn, do you have any idea why your brother decided to take a boat trip to Alaska?" asked Agent Rasmussen.

"No. I was totally unaware of his trip."

"You're trying to tell me that Richard travelled from Washington D.C. to your home state and didn't contact you?"

"That is correct."

"I find that hard to believe. When was the last time you talked to your brother?"

"He called me about two weeks ago from D.C. We talked about normal things like health, personal interests, vacation plans . . ."

"How did he seem mentally?"

"He seemed mentally fine—maybe a little bit tired. He said the senator had been running him ragged."

"What's your opinion of the senator?"

"I've only met the man once, and we talked for about thirty seconds. Consequently, I have no opinion. Richard was always careful to honor the confidentiality of his position, so I don't have any insight from him either. Can I ask what this has to do with his death?"

"No, you can't. There are national security issues involved, and we would like you to keep your nose out of the investigation," said Agent Rasmussen.

"I don't give a shit where you want me to keep my nose," exclaimed Michael. "As you know, I'm a federal prosecutor. I'm obviously not naïve when it comes to politics. But right now, I'm a grieving brother trying to wrap up the logistics of getting Richard's body back to Seattle and deal with the disposition of a million-dollar boat. Needless to say, I'm also interested in who killed him and why, but it's your job to figure that out. Don't try to bully me because it won't work. By the way, when will Richard's body be released?"

"The medical examiner in Kenai is doing the autopsy. The cause of death is pretty obvious, and it should be done later today. Blood and fluid samples have been sent to the FBI lab in Virginia. With some luck, the body can be available tomorrow afternoon," replied Agent Rasmussen.

"Ok. Do you guys need anything else from me?" said Michael.

"I guess not. We'll probably be in touch."

"I'll see you out," said Bob Stillwater as Michael got up to leave. At the front door, Bob added, "I'm sorry for your loss. And I'm sorry for the attitude of the assholes in blue suits."

"Thanks, I appreciate that," said Vandorn with a smile. "By the way, when will the boat be released from crime scene status?"

"Our forensics people are done with it, and the FBI forensic team is supposed to get here tomorrow morning," said Bob on his way out the door. "So, it may be free tomorrow afternoon. I can give you a call when it's available. Have a good night."

Chapter 8

Monday morning dawned bright and sunny, a welcome contrast to the dismal weather of the previous week. Calm winds and low tide exposed hundreds of acres of fragrant mudflats. The shallow, muddy shoreline surrounding the Homer spit with its rich intertidal fauna was known for attracting large numbers of shorebirds, providing an important refueling stop for some species during their spring and fall migrations. The glaciers across the bay glinted with the rising sun, and the snow-capped mountains glowed in the pastel pink of alpenglow. The busy harbor was waking up—big diesel engines rumbled from within the halibut charter boats while their crews prepared for the arrival of the day's customers.

Charlie and Kate emerged from their master suite in the former fish hold of the Shearwater. Tons of squirming salmon had been replaced by two lusty humans.

"What do you think is going to happen today?" asked Kate as she sat at the galley table and filled a bowl with granola. Charlie scooched in next to her with his coffee and a Homer News.

"I'm hoping we'll get a call from Michael Vandorn this morning so we can arrange a meeting and figure out where to go from here. He may also have information on a hidden compartment in the boat."

"Let's hope he finds something."

<hr>

Michael Vandorn spent the morning on the phone while reclining on the bed in his bare-bones hotel room. His first call was to the corporate headquarters for Nordhavn boats in Dana Point, California. After being passed from person to person, he was finally able to talk to the primary naval architect for the *Wonky*, a friendly guy named Wes Jones. He was more than willing to cooperate. Wes felt especially bad about Richard's death because he had worked closely with him on the boat's design details, and they had become friends.

"There is, indeed, a secret compartment which would be nearly impossible to find unless you knew where to look. It's behind the mirror mounted on the wall above the sink in the master suite head. It's solidly and seamlessly attached to the bulkhead. A small button under the sink behind the drainpipes trips a latching device, and the mirror swings out from the left. You should be able to feel the button by reaching under and behind the sink bowl."

"How big is the compartment?" asked Michael.

"It's about twelve inches deep, two feet wide, and maybe four feet tall, allowing storage of items from rifles to documents," replied the architect. "The size of the cavity is pretty much dictated by the boat's architecture and space between the bulkheads."

After the satisfying discussion with Wes Jones, Michael coordinated with a Kenai funeral home to arrange for Richard's body to be shipped to a family funeral home in Seattle after the release of the body by the FBI. The logistics were complicated, involving calls to airlines and customs authorities. As a further complication, Michael received several emails from Senator Strunk's office strongly suggesting that the body be buried in Washington, D.C. But Michael did not see the point and chose to ignore the missives from D.C. Somehow, the press found out that Michael was in Homer and hounded him with phone calls, which he also chose not to answer. The final call was to Charlie, suggesting they meet again in the evening, preferably at a quiet, private location.

The depressing hotel room began to feel claustrophobic to Michael, given his level of grief, so he decided to get out and explore the town. He thought that a drive might take his mind off the unfortunate situation. He was also curious whether the feds had him under surveillance.

As he was leaving the hotel, he noticed a dark-colored SUV several cars behind him. The vehicle appeared suspiciously clean for local transportation. He drove his rental through the Homer downtown area, then to the end of the spit across from the harbor. He parked and ate lunch at a seafood restaurant while keeping a close eye on his surroundings. He saw the same car waiting on the fringe of the restaurant parking lot. Obviously, the FBI agents were following him. But why exactly? There was nothing suspicious about his presence in Homer, given the circumstances. Plus, as a federal prosecutor, he had a high security clearance, and outranked most FBI team members. There was clearly something weird about the whole situation with his brother.

After finishing lunch, he considered his new found paranoia. It seemed logical that his calls might be monitored, so he stopped at a pharmacy and purchased a throw-away burner phone.

Michael called Charlie on his new phone and arranged to get together with Charlie and the other Moosketeers in the evening. They agreed that Michael would exit the hotel from a back door, get picked up by Charlie on a side street, and proceed to JB and Beverly's cabin.

CHAPTER 9

"**F**UCK!" MUTTERED STANLEY KRUPP as he tripped over yet another horizontal alder trunk. He was bushwhacking along the north bank of the Kenai River, looking for a good sniper nest location. Since Stanley was the only conspirator familiar with southcentral Alaska, the job of advance planning fell to him. The ideal site had to have a number of characteristics—remote location, good sight lines to the river, enough vegetation to screen the shooter, and relatively easy access to allow the assassin to escape. Stanley was once a sniper in Iraq, so he was sensitive to the sniper's needs. However, it was unlikely that Stanley would do the actual shooting. Some things needed to be contracted.

He had managed to bribe a junior staffer in VP Taylor's office to obtain Taylor's Alaska vacation itinerary. Stanley discovered that the vice president was planning two guided fishing trips on the Kenai River—one based from a motorboat on the lower river for various salmon species and another in a drift boat on the upper river for rainbow trout. A quick review of Google Earth satellite imagery confirmed what he already knew, which was that much of the lower river was lined by recreational cabins on both sides. Much of the upper river closely paralleled a major highway, effectively eliminating long reaches from consideration as assassination corridors.

But accessing the wilder sections of the river presented other logistical difficulties. Much of southern Alaska is not conducive to cross-country travel because of boggy terrain, dense brush, interlocking alders, spiny devil's club, and fallen trees. Stanley recalled an article in a newspaper from years ago describing the adventures of two German hikers who had bragged about their plans to walk across the state from south to north. The gist of the story was that they made it only a few miles before giving up, accompanied by great embarrassment.

During his review of the river, Stanley settled on an undeveloped portion of the middle river west of Skilac Lake for his initial reconnaissance. He knew from his research that one of the guided fishing trips booked by the vice president would likely fish along the reach—probably motoring upstream and drifting back downstream. Stanley parked his SUV on an unused road on the outskirts of a river subdivision and began hiking using a GPS map device to guide him to a spot on the river that looked promising.

He reached the north bank of the river after hiking for about an hour and a half and walked along the eroding cut bank, looking for the ideal vantage point. The strikingly-colored, blue-green river flowed about forty feet below him. The water was moving fast, but not fast enough to create white water. The distance from the top of the bank to the far side of the river was about three hundred feet—an easy shot for an experienced sniper, even when the motion of the boat was factored into the equation.

He came to a location where the vegetation on the top of the bank consisted of a dense growth of young spruce trees, resulting in a low, impenetrable canopy about three feet off the ground. Stanley had to crawl beneath the sharp, pointed Sitka spruce needles to reach the edge of the bank and get a clear view of the river. While inconvenient, the situation was ideal for hiding a gunman from the river and also from above. Stanley thought it was likely that security for the vice president's fishing excursion would include surveillance by helicopter or a drone, so dense overhead cover was essential. Using his old ranger knife, he trimmed the small lower branches to clear a comfortable space for a person to recline on the edge of the bank.

Stanley marked the approach to his selected location with surveyor's flagging and wrote the coordinates in his notebook. In addition, he marked a waypoint and route on his GPS map device, which could be mailed directly to the contracted gunman.

Since it was early afternoon on a beautiful day, Stanley decided to hang out for a while to get a feeling for the area. He crawled into his sniper's nest, rested his head on his pack, and stared at the river. After about five minutes, a boat appeared, drifting downstream from left to right. The boat floated smoothly past his location, suggesting that excess motion would not interfere with the ability to get a good shot at passengers in a boat.

Stanley opened his pack, removed a ham and cheese sandwich, and ate lunch. As he ate, he watched a bald eagle swoop down to the river, grab a six-inch fish, carry it to a tree branch, and proceed to rip it apart. Shortly after, a brown bear emerged from the willows onto the gravel bar on the far side of the river and began to eat the carcass of an early-run salmon. Stanley fell asleep.

Awaking with a start, Stanley realized he had been asleep for about an hour. The bear was gone, and shadows were lengthening. He reluctantly headed back to his vehicle, again timing the trip. He encountered no people on the return trip through the river subdivision. All in all, he was happy with the results of his excursion.

CHAPTER 10

At about five o'clock on the same day as Stanley Krupp's reconnaissance adventure and one day after arriving in Homer, Michael Vandorn met Charlie and Kate behind the hotel as planned and drove to Beverly's cabin in Charlie's car. No feds were seen *en route*. After introductions and minimal small talk, the conversation turned to the death of Richard Vandorn.

"We're very sorry for your loss," said Beverly. "If you'd rather not talk about events in Homer, we can wait."

"My priority right now is to try and figure out what the heck is going on, but thanks for asking. Can you guys give me some idea of your backgrounds?"

Beverly described her career with the DEA and subsequent life trajectory change after meeting JB and moving to Homer. JB was, of course, more circumspect. Since Michael had a high-security clearance, JB could fill him in on the basics of his early life in the intelligence community without providing any details of assignments and such. Charlie described the cooperation between the four Mooseketeers and law enforcement during the Aldo Fenstrom drug syndicate affair and the murders related to an ill-fated rare earth mine project. Beverly described the launch of her detective agency and the fact that Kate's hacking skills were playing a starring role.

"Wow, you guys are impressive," said Michael as JB handed him a beer. "I could use you on my staff in Seattle. Does anybody have any idea why Richard was here and why he was killed?"

"We don't have much in the way of helpful information," replied JB as he munched on a chip, dripping salsa on his T-shirt du jour featuring the Grateful Dead on an early tour. "Your office is probably more plugged in to what is going on with Senator Strunk, or at least may be able to find out."

"I definitely intend to use whatever resources I can muster," added Michael. "But Washington D.C. can be an insular place, and I'm not too optimistic about finding anything through the main justice department or the senate. I've talked to Richard's secretary from time to time. She seems cooperative and may be able to help. I may try calling her at home."

"If Richard's death is related to something going on with Senator Strunk, then his secretary may also be in danger," Kate added. "Contacting her might add to her jeopardy."

"Yeah. I've been thinking about that. I'll try to come up with a way to contact her without anyone knowing," said Michael.

"Were you able to find out anything about a secret compartment on the boat?" asked Charlie.

"Yes. There is one, and I know where it is. The marine architect who designed the boat was very cooperative and eager to help. Hopefully, the FBI forensics people will finish up quickly, and we can get a look without them around. They're supposed to arrive tomorrow morning. Also, if the boat is released from crime scene status, I intend to move aboard. It's a lot nicer and less expensive than my hotel room."

"How long do you plan to stay in Homer?" asked Kate.

"I guess it partly depends on arrangements for my brother's funeral on San Juan Island. I took a ten-day leave from my job, so I'll be here for a couple of days."

Michael began to relax after a couple of beers, and the conversation turned to more general topics, such as life in Homer, fishing, and other Alaska topics.

At ten o'clock, Charlie and Kate dropped Michael at the back of the hotel, where they had picked him up. As he opened the door to his room, he checked the hair he had placed on the top of the door as an entry trap and discovered that someone had been in his room. *Crap!* They obviously knew that he had snuck out. Plus, it seemed likely that his room was now bugged. *Why are they so interested in me?*

———◆———

In another hotel room on a different floor, Agent Rasmussen and his deputy, Agent Clark, were kicking back, splitting a bottle of Crown Royal. Agent Clark's appearance was pretty much the opposite of his boss—he was tall and thin with a narrow face and wavy brown hair, whereas Agent Rasmussen was of medium height and stout with a pudgy face and shaved head. The two were often referred to in the service as Tweedle Dum and Tweedle Dee.

"Why do you think Vandorn is sneaking around?" asked Rasmussen.

"I don't know. We may be making too much of this. He may be sneaking because he knows we've been following him, and he doesn't like to be followed. I'd be doing the same thing if I knew someone was tailing me, whether or not I had something to hide. Plus, we may get ourselves into trouble for surveilling a federal prosecutor without a good reason, not to mention the fact that the guy's brother was just killed."

"Yeah, maybe. Still, I wonder where he went tonight."

"Well, we could ask him."

"Let's wait and see if we get any information from the bug in his room."

"Do you think we'll get anything useful from the boat when our forensic people arrive in the morning?"

"I doubt it. The Alaska troopers have probably found most of what there is to find. But maybe something will turn up."

"What I'm wondering is why are we even here? And why send four FBI agents? There isn't that much to investigate," said Agent Clark.

"I was told that Vandorn's murder qualified as a national security threat and that we should follow any Alaska-based leads that we can find," replied Agent Rasmussen.

"What if there aren't any leads?"

"Yeah, that would be a problem. That's why I'm holding on to Michael Vandorn as a person of interest. He's all we've got."

Chapter 11

Tuesday morning saw a flurry of activity at the Homer docks. The FBI team, now fortified by two forensic specialists, paraded down the pier to the *Wonky*. Donning hazmat suits, the forensic guys entered the boat and proceeded to examine every surface, search every drawer, vacuum every bit of floor, and spread fingerprint dust everywhere. When they finished, the boat was a mess.

"So, what did you find?" asked Agent Rasmussen.

"Not much," answered Doc Waverly, the chief scientist. "A couple sets of fingerprints, other than Vandorn's, we haven't had a chance to check on yet. We should get results on the prints in a few hours. Blood spatter was pretty limited—some fine droplets on the cabin door near where the bullet was found, which would be expected with a through-and-through wound. No surprise there. No more documents or written materials beyond those found by the troopers. Basically, I don't think the boat is going to help your investigation very much."

"Great," said Agent Clark. "What do we do now? We still have no idea why Richard Vandorn felt compelled to drive a boat fifteen hundred miles to Homer, and we have no leads."

"Yeah. We need to regroup and figure out where we are going to go from here." Turning to Doc Waverly, Agent Rasmussen said, "So, if you guys are done with the boat, I think I'll wrap up the crime scene and let Vandorn do what he wants with it. We don't need the hassle of dealing with a million-dollar yacht, which is apparently currently owned by a federal prosecutor."

———◆———

"I know you guys were in my room!" said Michael Vandorn as he paced restlessly in the trooper conference room. "Why the hell would you do that? Also, I found the bug that you put there. I could theoretically get you fired. Would you like to explain why you're surveilling me and why Washington is so interested in this situation?"

"We were told that Richard Vandorn's murder was a very sensitive national security matter, and we should use any means necessary to catch the killer and acquire any relevant documents," replied Agent Rasmussen.

"Relevant to what?" asked Michael.

"We don't actually know. Our boss said that we would recognize important information when we see it. By the way, where did you go last night?"

"Not that it is any of your business, but I was invited to a friend's for dinner. We had drinks and pleasant conversation, and then I came back to the hotel," replied Michael as he got up to go. "Has Richard's boat been released from crime scene status yet?"

"Yeah, we're done with it."

"OK, I'm going to move from the hotel to the boat for a couple of days until I finish making arrangements for the transport of Richard's body," Michael said as he left.

Michael checked out of the hotel and moved his stuff into the *Wonky*, entering the salon, where the large pool of dried blood was still evident. The sight made him queasy and brought back memories of his childhood, playing and fighting with his brother. Visions of the past kept replaying in his head. Both brothers were smart and ambitious, but while Michael was handsome and athletic, Richard had been short, prematurely bald, and sported a large nose. Richard compensated for his looks by being very outgoing and friendly. In short, he was a natural politician.

Michael spent the next few hours cleaning up the blood and the mess the forensic crew had made. Even though he had only been out on the *Wonky* a few times with Richard, Michael loved this boat. He started to think about whether he was up to the task of driving the boat back home. He would need to take a crash course in piloting a small yacht. But he was unsure whether he could ever be comfortable given its history.

He fixed himself a sandwich by scrounging leftovers in the galley and watched satellite TV until dark. At about eleven o'clock, Michael went out on the deck and looked around. The harbor was totally quiet. Locking the doors and returning to the master stateroom, he entered the small head and looked at the mirror above the sink. It appeared to be solidly integral with the bulkhead behind it. He opened the sink cabinet, reached under and behind the sink, and felt around for the secret button. He missed it on his first try and began to think that the marine architect was full of shit, but he tried again and managed to find a toggle switch up against the sink flange. He flipped the switch, followed by a buzzing sound, and the mirror swung away from the wall.

Michael peered into the dark space using the light from his phone flashlight. Inside the compartment were several items: a scoped bolt-action rifle in a big game caliber, a .40 caliber Smith & Wesson semi-automatic handgun, ammunition and extra magazines, a bundle of cash, and a diary-size notebook. He removed the handgun and put it under the pillow on the queen-sized bed. Although he had no idea what the notebook was all about, he had a feeling that its contents might provide hints to the cause of Richard's death. It seemed possible that he might also be in danger because of his snooping. Michael hoped the killer was satisfied that there was no useful information on the boat.

Nevertheless, he locked the boat and pulled shades over the portholes in the master cabin. Michael began to go through the diary as he lay on the bed. The handwriting was clearly his brother's and just as illegible as ever.

The first few pages seemed to be scheduling notes, appointment times, and meeting locations. But on the fifth page were the words "Project Nemesis" underlined three times, followed by a list of three names, none of which Michael recognized. The first name was Stanley Krupp, with Alaska and Washington, D.C. scrawled after his name. The second name was John Melman, with Homer, Alaska added after the name. Finally, a Homer connection, thought Michael. The third name was Dick Whelan from Washington State. Following the name list were some barely legible notations—keywords and phrases similar to college lecture notes. Among the words that Michael recognized were "Vice President Taylor," "assassination," and "Alaska fishing trip."

Crap, thought Michael. *Unfortunately, things are starting to make some sense.*

Michael was tired and needed to sleep, but as he lay in the comfortable bed, his mind would not let go of the fact that he had no idea what he should do now. He did not know whether he could trust the FBI guys, and it seemed likely that Senator Strunk was part of a conspiracy, given his brother's involvement. One possibility was to take the information to people he trusted and worked with in the Washington State Federal Prosecutor's Office. But the wheels turned very slowly in the federal bureaucracy, and he felt that events might be moving too quickly. For some reason, he had more trust in his new Homer friends than in his acquaintances in the law enforcement community. He would call Charlie in the morning.

Michael finally drifted off to sleep, lulled by raindrops on the cabin roof.

CHAPTER 12

THE NEXT MORNING, THE *Shearwater* bobbed in the small waves offshore from the town of English Bay near Flat Island, just outside Kachemak Bay. The boat was anchored in one hundred feet of water, and the five occupants were ostensibly halibut fishing. In response to Michael Vandorn's early morning call requesting a private discussion, they decided that the middle of the bay offered adequate privacy. As an added bonus, they could fish at the same time. Kate took a sick day from work so the full force of the four Mooseketeers could be present. They each had heavy halibut rods and deep-sea reels with eighty-pound line. At the end of each line was a wire leader with a one-pound lead ball that bounced along the bottom, trailing a hook baited with herring.

Puffins and murres from nearby nest colonies swam around the boat, diving for small fish. It was amusing to watch the birds in the clear water, essentially flying while submerged, using their wings to help with propulsion. Occasionally, a bird would surface with a fish crosswise in its beak, looking too big to swallow. But a few seconds of manipulation turned the fish so that it could slither lengthwise down the bird's gullet.

"So," Charlie said as he looked at Michael, "What have you learned that inspired you to call this meeting? "

"I spent last night on the *Wonky* and found the secret compartment, thanks to Charlie's suggestion. The compartment had a couple of guns, some money, and a notebook inside. The book contained notes handwritten by my brother during various meetings or maybe things he overheard through thin walls. Richard was an obsessive note-taker. Most of his scribblings were innocuous schedule reminders and other daily stuff, but one page stood out. I frankly don't know what to do with the information." Michael pulled up a photo on his phone and passed it around.

"Holy shit," said Beverly.

"I second that," agreed JB.

"This is too much of a coincidence," said Kate.

"What is too much of a coincidence?" asked Michael.

"As it turns out, we have some information of our own which coincides with your brother's notes. There's obviously no need to keep it secret any longer," added Charlie as he retrieved the so-called top-secret document from a galley drawer and handed it to Michael. Michael stared in amazement.

JB summarized the mystery document that had fallen into their hands as Vandorn paged through it.

"Exactly how did you get this document?" asked Michael.

"It's probably better if you don't know the answer to that, although we mostly did not commit any illegal acts," said JB. "I guess the point is the five of us may be the only non-conspirators who know about this. So, what do we do now? Involving law enforcement seems sort of tricky since we don't know who to trust."

"Michael, what do you think of getting the Justice Department involved in getting to the bottom of the conspiracy?" asked Charlie as he rebaited his hook.

"The FBI team in Homer has been acting as if they are getting instructions from someone in D.C., but my feeling is that the agents in Homer are pretty much clueless. If some members of the FBI are involved, there may well be Justice Department involvement as well, since we're basically part of the same organization. I take it you guys have already been thinking about what to do," said Michael.

"We've been thinking about it, but we haven't had any solid information to follow up on. At least now we have some names to deal with," said Kate as she reeled in to check her bait. "It gives us a place to start, assuming we're going to pursue this on our own."

"I think we can assume that Richard came up here to try and find out what was going on with Project Nemesis," said Michael. "The fact that he was murdered suggests someone knew he was coming. We could all be in danger if we dig into this."

"I guess that means we have to be extra sneaky," said JB. "As far as I know, the FBI guys and the conspirators haven't zeroed in on us, so maybe we can stay under the radar."

"I'm going back to Seattle in two days to deal with Richard's funeral, so I'll be out of the way," added Michael. "Also, I think the agents are going back soon since they've run into a dead end up here. That should leave you on your own to do what you want. I've been thinking about possibly taking a leave from work. I'm apparently the new owner of a very nice yacht—I might as well take advantage of it. The bottom line is, I will probably be back up here in a few days. I suggest we buy some burner phones so we can communicate without others listening."

"OK. So, meanwhile, we can dig into the names from Richard's notes and see what we find," said Charlie. "We may be able to get additional information by surveilling the guy from Homer."

"Somebody in Homer or nearby is clearly dangerous and desperate enough to commit murder in a crowded harbor. It would sure be nice if we could figure out who that is," Beverly added as she let out more line.

"Whoa!" exclaimed Michael as his rod bent almost in half, and line started spooling out of his reel.

"I think you've got a good-sized halibut. Keep the rod tip up and tighten the drag a little," Charlie said.

The fish kept running until the line was almost gone from the reel, but then seemed to stop.

"Oh, oh. He's turning around! Reel back in as fast as you can," Kate yelled. "Don't leave any slack!"

The fish began taking out line again, but then the line suddenly went limp.

"I think you lost him," said Charlie.

"Wow, that was exciting," exclaimed Michael. "I could get used to this. How big do you think the fish was?"

"At least a hundred pounds—maybe bigger," replied Charlie as Michael reeled his line in. The line had broken above the leader, suggesting that a large halibut was now swimming around with a hook in its mouth and a wire leader trailing behind.

"What do you do with a fish that big when you get it to the boat?" asked Michael.

"We shoot it in the water before hauling it aboard. A big halibut flopping around in the boat tends to break things and hurt people."

"You're kidding," replied Michael.

"Nope," said Charlie. "Things can get exciting out here."

It was late afternoon, and the sun was nearing the tops of the rugged Alaska Range peaks to the northwest, glinting off the water, creating an appearance like liquid mercury.

"It's probably time to call it a day," said Charlie as he began to stow the fishing gear. The Shearwater weighed anchor and headed back to Homer.

"Hey, Charlie," asked Michael. "What would you think of teaching me how to run a forty-foot yacht so I can get the Nordhavn back home?"

"I'd be glad to, but the systems on the *Wonky* are more high-tech than my boat, so I'd have to do some learning myself. But it's a way cool boat. Sounds like fun."

CHAPTER 13

O N Thursday morning, the tide was low, the wind was calm, the sky was mostly clear, and the temperature was mild. The snow-capped mountains across Kachemak Bay gleamed in the sunlight. Such days were too rare in Homer to waste by staying inside. Kate sat on the back deck of the *Shearwater* with her computer on her lap. Earlier, she had called her boss at FlashFrozen and asked for another sick day. He was well aware that she was not sick, but played along. She was a valuable employee, and he had a secret crush on her—not that it would do him any good.

She started her search with John Melman, the Homer resident mentioned in Richard Vandorn's notes. The name sounded vaguely familiar, and she wondered whether he had been present at some public meetings that she attended. He lived in one of the scruffier subdivisions off East End Road, not too far from JB and Beverly. Kate obtained Melman's address and mobile phone number using one of the many location websites. He was active on social media, spotlighting his hunting and fishing prowess. Photos showed that he was of average height, somewhat overweight, with dirty brown hair, a full brown beard, a square face, and a perpetual scowl. He had a full sleeve of tattoos on his left arm featuring unusual designs similar to tattoos Kate had seen on Māori men in New Zealand. His fashion choice was limited to camo. As far as Kate could tell, Melman did not have a regular job, although he earned some money as a fishing guide in the summer. There was no indication that Melman was married or had a girlfriend.

A few dialogues on Facebook suggested that Melman was a member of a local group calling for Alaska to secede. There was a lot of whining about an unjust world and the inability of average people to get a fair shake. The discussions were mild and did not raise red flags of violence. Kate felt that communications about actual plots, if they exist, would most likely be in a dark web chat room or encrypted email. Accordingly, she searched the dark web for references to Project Nemesis or John Melman using software provided by her brother. She found some suspicious sites, but the encryption blocked entry. A search of criminal records showed only two traffic tickets and an old misdemeanor marijuana charge—nothing of major significance.

Having reached a dead end with Melman, Kate switched gears to the other name associated with Alaska, Stanley Krupp. Krupp was much more interesting. Google had several pages of entries related to him. Apparently, he was a Washington, D.C. insider and lobbyist, hobnobbing with various important people. He had a residence in Washington, D.C. as well as a cabin in the Caribou Hills, near Homer. Krupp graduated from Harvard and Yale Law as well as the Army Rangers, and so had the ideal education for relating to the powerful people in D.C. He was on the board of directors for a lobbying firm called Gentle Persuasion. A Facebook post from Krupp's adolescent granddaughter indicated that he was currently in Alaska, enjoying recreational activities. He was apparently divorced from the mother of his daughter. Kate thought it was interesting that Krupp was already in Alaska. It seemed logical that he might coordinate the Alaskan activities of the Project Nemesis group.

Stanley Krupp's education and knowledge of machinations in the Washington, D.C. political ecosystem suggested to Kate that he might be the leader of Project Nemesis. John Melman, on the other hand, was most likely tapped as a sympathetic local willing to help out—maybe do the dirty work.

The third name mentioned in Vandorn's notes was Dick Whelan from Seattle. Whelan seemed to be a very low-profile guy with little presence on the internet or social media—not even an email address. All Kate could find was a street address near Lake Washington. The photo on his driver's license showed a man with a crooked nose, full red beard, and neatly trimmed light brown hair.

------◆------

Kate was finishing lunch as Charlie returned from a grocery shopping expedition. "So, what did super hacker find this morning?"

"Nothing too earth-shaking," answered Kate. "Melman, the local guy, is most likely not a key instigator, but he may be providing local coordination and a sympathetic ear to the cause, whatever that may be. He lives out near JB and Beverly in one of the unzoned, do-it-yourself subdivisions. He's probably our most direct link to whatever is going on. Stanley Krupp's an Ivy League Washington insider and lobbyist who happens to have a cabin near the Caribou Hills. He's there right now, according to his granddaughter on Facebook. It seems likely that he's a major player given his credentials."

"OK. JB should be here in a minute, and we can talk about where to go from here. Beverly's dealing with private investigator stuff this afternoon."

The *Shearwater* shuddered and listed to starboard as JB swung aboard, grabbing the rigging like in an old pirate movie. His long arms reminded Kate of an orangutan. His dramatic entrance was punctuated by his Grateful Dead T-shirt du jour, which featured a ghostly Jerry Garcia standing on a cloud with his guitar surrounded by a purple aura.

"Is it too early for a beer?" asked JB.

"No problem. I'll just add it to your tab," quipped Charlie.

"You're not really keeping a tab, are you?" asked JB as he opened the fridge.

"I'll send you a bill when it hits a thousand dollars."

"Yeah, yeah. So where are we in our new investigation?"

Kate briefed JB on the results of her morning activities with emphasis on the one Homer resident, John Melman. She pulled up Google Earth and found Melman's address with no problem. The satellite view indicated that Melman's small house was located at the end of a road in a relatively secluded area. Like most of the houses in the subdivision, Melman's cabin appeared to be a small, self-constructed, one-story abode. It was surrounded by dense forest, broken only by the narrow gravel driveway.

"It looks like it would be pretty easy to access the area without being seen," suggested JB. "I could use some of the same surveillance gear I used on our last adventure. It would actually be a lot easier since the area is nearby, and my recording device could be accessed by regular cell phone rather than satellite phone."

JB had used a voice-activated recording device, the contents of which could be downloaded by simply calling the device. The recorder had been used to monitor phone conversations at a remote mining camp and helped to provide essential evidence of the corrupt intent of the miners.

"We should probably start by getting a handle on Melman's routine—when he's home or not home," added Charlie. "I guess that assumes he actually has a schedule. If not, we can watch the place until he leaves. JB, do you feel the urge to camp out in the woods and watch Mr. Melman?"

"I think I can probably find a gap in my schedule." JB was not currently employed, and it was a mystery how he managed to survive. Kate and Charlie suspected he had some money squirreled away from activities in his mysterious past. Kate had pumped Beverly for information regarding JB's finances, but she had been sworn to secrecy and was not talking.

"Kate, can you find out what kind of car Melman drives?" asked Charlie.

"No problem. I'll do it right now." Kate spent about ten minutes tapping away at her laptop. "It looks like he drives an ancient Chevy Blazer, and his license tags are overdue." She wrote down the plate number and handed it to JB. She also printed Melman's driver's license with his photo. A full brown beard, shaggy hair, and glasses obscured his face. An unidentifiable tattoo was visible on the right side of his neck.

"I don't think I want to know how you did that," said Charlie.

"It's probably best you don't," replied Kate.

"I can do an initial reconnaissance of the area tonight. Maybe Beverly will go with me," said JB.

"Sounds romantic," added Kate.

"Yeah, sneaking through the woods always turns me on," JB said.

———◆———

ONCE AGAIN, JB AND Beverly were bouncing around in JB's old jeep. The rough dirt road leading to John Melman's cabin left a lot to be desired, especially after the hard rain of the last two weeks. Analysis of Google Earth satellite imagery for the area near Melman's place suggested a possible approach from an unused adjacent road, which would keep them out of sight. A short hike through the woods brought them to the edge of the target property as it was starting to get dark. A red and white Chevy Blazer with many rust spots was parked near the front door.

A bark beetle infestation shortly after the turn of the millennium had killed almost all of the mature Sitka spruce adjacent to Kachemak Bay. Since then, much of the Homer area had been repopulated by young spruce with greater resistance to the bugs, replacing the old guard. These stands of small spruce were dense and provided good cover for JB and Beverly, although presenting a rather ugly, scrubby appearance. They could easily move to within forty feet of the cabin without being seen. Lights in the cabin were on, and every once in a while, Melman could be glimpsed as he walked past a window. It seemed like he was cooking dinner.

"There's not much more we can do tonight," said JB. "It looks like it should be pretty easy to watch the place during the day and plant a listening device as soon as Melman leaves. We can try and do that tomorrow, assuming he doesn't stay home all day."

CHAPTER 14

JB AND BEVERLY AWOKE early Friday morning to dismal skies and light rain. JB filled a backpack with an assortment of spy gadgets, along with food and other items they might need while hanging out in the bushes, waiting for Melman to leave his cabin. A couple of years earlier, JB had stumbled across an ad for high-tech surveillance equipment, some of which looked really cool, albeit only marginally legal. So, on a whim, he had ordered several items, not really expecting to use any of them. But, as it turned out, the gadgets proved to be essential during their previous investigation of mine-related murders across the inlet. Now it seemed like they might be put to use again.

JB rolled his eyes as Beverly put a twelve-pack of Twinkies into her pack. Beverly had been on many stakeouts during her tenure with the Drug Enforcement Agency and found them incredibly boring. Twinkie breaks had been a mainstay of her stake-out paraphernalia for many years. Normally, she ate one Twinkie every half hour to make the time go faster.

Shortly after sunrise, they donned rain gear and drove the short distance to Melman's subdivision. They hid the jeep in the bushes off one of the subdivision roads, trekked through the dense spruce near Melman's cabin, and settled in at the observation spot identified by JB on their earlier reconnaissance. A tarp and a blanket on the ground kept them dry and reasonably comfortable.

The cabin was dark when they arrived, and Melman's ancient Chevy Blazer sat forlornly in the driveway. JB took advantage of the dim light and lack of activity in the cabin to plant a magnetic tracking device under the Blazer. About half an hour after the arrival of JB and Beverly, a light went on in the cabin, and Melman could be seen moving around through the windows. The nosy duo took this as a good sign that their target might leave for some unknown destination fairly soon, but, unfortunately, it seemed like he was simply an early riser and not going anywhere. After an hour, Beverly ate her second Twinkie and discovered to her annoyance that JB was fast asleep. Three Twinkies later, Melman emerged from the front door, got in his vehicle and left.

JB woke as soon as the Blazer left.

"How do you do that?" asked Beverly.

"Years of practice," replied JB.

After waiting about five minutes, the couple approached the cabin and entered via the unlocked front door. A quick look around explained the lack of concern about break-ins—there was nothing to steal. To describe the cabin as bare bones would be an understatement. The one large room contained only an old sofa, a second-hand wood stove, an ancient TV on concrete blocks, a mattress on the floor, a short plywood kitchen counter, and minimal kitchen utensils. The floor and three of the walls were bare plywood. One wall and the rafters overhead remained unfinished, giving the room a pink tinge because of the exposed insulation. No books or other reading materials were present except for two soldier-of-fortune magazines on the floor. Melman was clearly not an intellectual genius. Cold weather gear hung from nails in the wall, and miscellaneous clothing was scattered on the floor. Interior decoration consisted solely of a calendar featuring hunting scenes, mostly photos of hunters proudly posing with various sad-looking deceased creatures.

JB scanned the cabin to find a good place to install his voice-activated recorder—basically a modified smartphone allowing the recordings to be accessed by calling the device and downloading to another phone. JB settled on a location for the gadget in the rafters adjacent to a light fixture junction box, making it almost invisible from below. Since the cabin was only one room, he figured the recorder would pick up any conversation within the building. Importantly, one side of any phone conversations would also be heard.

Meanwhile, Beverly searched for any information relating to the Project Nemesis conspiracy. Next to the ratty mattress was a small side table that looked like something that might have been constructed during a junior high shop class. A little drawer in the table contained a tangled nest of sticky notes with barely legible writing, most of which seemed to be names and phone numbers. Beverly laid the notes on top of the table, photographed them with her phone, and returned them to the drawer, trying to replicate the original messy condition. Also, in the drawer was a jumbo-size pack of condoms.

"Wow. This guy's into some serious wishful thinking," said Beverly as she held up the brick-size package of prophylactics. "His living conditions suggest he's not the most desirable human being."

"Yeah. Maybe he made a recent trip to Costco," replied JB.

Lifting the mattress, Beverly discovered a 9-mm semiautomatic handgun. She photographed the gun and its serial number.

"You would think anyone hiding a gun would find a more imaginative hiding place."

"Yeah, Melman doesn't seem too bright. Let's get out of here," said JB. "That was way too easy."

Beverly looked at her watch, surprised they had only been in the cabin for ten minutes. It seemed much longer. They carefully exited the cabin and made their way back to the Jeep.

—— ◆ ——

While JB and Beverly were playing spy, Kate sat in her office at FlashFrozen Seafoods, rapidly typing on her computer. She was supposed to be working on the company payroll, but, in actuality, was reviewing land records for the Kenai Peninsula Borough to see whether she could find Stanley Krupp's cabin. She obviously hoped that it would be recorded in his real name. The land records were public information, so her activities were actually legal, but tedious. The borough's system was poorly organized, and cross-referencing property locations with names was much more difficult than it needed to be.

Eventually, she found a five-acre plot adjacent to a small lake with a modest cabin registered to Stanley J. Krupp. The property was in the middle of nowhere, about forty miles from Homer. Most of the surrounding land was owned by the State of Alaska. Switching to Google Earth, she looked at the satellite view of the property. The log cabin was the only human habitation within several square miles. Kate noted a cleared strip of land near the cabin—probably an airstrip. Land access would likely be difficult during the thawed season. Kate zoomed out on the Google Earth image and looked for the nearest trails to the cabin. A maze of four-wheeler trails provided access to the nearby Caribou Hills for various recreational pursuits, but the closest approach to Krupp's cabin was about two miles away.

Investigating Krupp was going to be challenging and time-consuming. It would probably take most of a day to access the cabin using a combination of four-wheel ATV and foot travel. It might be necessary to camp out for at least one night. And there were no guarantees of finding useful information.

———◆———

IN THE LATE AFTERNOON, the Mooseketeers regrouped again in the galley of the *Shearwater*. As usual, beer and potato chips were the center of attention. JB, Beverly, and Kate described their various snooping activities and the information gathered thus far.

"So, do we have a record of Melman's travels today?" asked Charlie.

"Yeah, the tracker's working great," replied JB as he opened the app on his phone. "After leaving his cabin, Melman stopped at McDonald's for breakfast, then went to the internet café downtown and stayed for about an hour. After that, he went back home for several hours. At about three o'clock, he left and went to Gertie's Tavern, where he currently resides."

"Do we have any way of finding out what he did at the internet café?" asked JB.

"Basically, no," added Kate.

"I queried the recorder in Melman's cabin a few minutes ago, but there was nothing on it yet," said JB.

"Ok," said Charlie. "I guess we have a couple of tasks, should we choose to accept our assignment of saving the country. We can try to get to Krupp's cabin, plant another listening device, and see what else we can find. Also, we need to get with the Super Trooper and see what's going on with the investigation into Richard Vandorn's murder. Michael Vandorn will be getting back to Homer the day after tomorrow, so we can follow up and coordinate with him."

"How about if Charlie and I try to get to Krupp's cabin on Monday?" suggested JB as he reached for another beer. "Beverly has PI work to deal with, and Kate is practically supporting us all since she actually has a job."

"We may be able to get an idea whether Krupp is currently at the cabin since he has been posting to Facebook about his travels with his adolescent daughter," said Kate, accessing Facebook on her laptop. "I think we're in luck. It sounds like he will be returning to Washington, D.C. tomorrow and then back to Alaska in about a week."

"I guess we'll need an ATV and a trailer to transport it. I can arrange for that," said Charlie. "I'm somewhat familiar with the area, so I'll try to plot a route that gets us close to Kruppville."

"Meanwhile, I'll keep tracking Melman's car and listening for conversations in his cabin," added JB as he chugged the remainder of his beer. "I think I'll also try to contact my old boss in Washington, D.C. and see what ideas he might have."

Chapter 15

JB was, by far, the most mysterious member of the Mooseketeers. His full name was Johann Sebastian Bachman. He did not know whether his parents were being ironic when they named him, or whether they genuinely admired the dead composer. He had limped into Homer Harbor in his beat-up thirty-two-foot sailboat in 2008 and set up residence in the boat slip next to Charlie's. The *Otterly Ridiculous* had not left the harbor since its arrival and had become increasingly cluttered and rundown. As a live-aboard, JB accumulated lots of stuff. The decks sported an array of potted plants, buoys, ropes, and assorted junk. At one time, the front deck featured a six-foot-tall marijuana plant named Fred. But the subsequent legalization of pot rendered Fred obsolete, and he was consumed at a large beach party.

JB's appearance somehow seemed consistent with the clutter of his sailboat. He was awkwardly tall and lanky but moved with an unexpected athletic grace. His light brown hair was always disheveled, sticking up as if in a constant state of static cling. In short, he looked like a combination of Ichabod Crane and Albert Einstein. His fashion repertoire was simple—jeans and one of his many T-shirts with a Grateful Dead theme.

JB and Charlie soon became friends, and Charlie marveled at JB's quick, but unusual, mind. Out of curiosity, Charlie had looked up

JB on the internet and was surprised to find very little information except for a burst of postings during the period immediately before his Homer arrival. Apparently, JB had been a professor of political science at a Southern California university until he was fired because of an affair with a student. The student newspaper made it clear that the students were not happy that the popular professor was being removed. There was a record of JB having obtained a PH.D. in his late twenties, but no record of his existence prior to that time.

For reasons incomprehensible to Charlie, JB had a knack for attracting young women from Homer's counterculture, whom he would take to his bed for a few weeks, always followed by an amicable breakup. Apparently, he gained a reputation as a sort of hippie guru. But JB's infatuation with seemingly strait-laced DEA agent, Beverly Milford, ended his carefree lifestyle and resulted in one of the strangest couples imaginable. JB was coerced into abandoning his beloved, but cramped, sailboat, and, after much discussion, he moved into Beverly's more comfortable cabin. Such is love.

During the group adventures over the previous three years, it became obvious that JB had unusual skills and training. JB eventually revealed that he had been recruited at the age of eighteen for a career in intelligence and clandestine operations. During the eight years between ages of eighteen and twenty-six, he underwent intensive training ranging from weapons systems and martial arts to languages and cultural studies. He told Charlie that he had come to the realization that some of the activities of the black ops group were immoral, and he wanted out. He made an arrangement with his old boss, Karl, to stay in contact. Normally, such contacts were forbidden, but Karl had a special affection for JB. Plus, JB knew where all the literal and figurative bodies were buried.

At six o'clock the next morning, JB fixed himself a cup of coffee and sat at his small desk in Beverly's cabin. Beverly was still sleeping soundly. He reached for a book on twentieth-century political movements from his bookshelf, turned to page 121, and extracted a note with a long alphanumeric code. Opening a website that displayed only a Celtic symbol, he typed in the code, which resulted in an encrypted email form. Using the form, he transmitted copies of the Project Nemesis document introduction and requested a reply via encrypted phone.

It did not take long. A few minutes later, JB's phone rang.

"Good morning, Johann," said Karl. "I see you've gotten yourself in the shit again. Where the hell did you get this?"

"It's probably best if you don't know the details. It sorta accidentally fell into our laps, but it probably originally came from Clarence Ayre's apartment and was in an official TOP SECRET folder. But there was no chain of custody, no names were mentioned, and it clearly is not a sanctioned document. The document describes a plot to kill the vice president during a fishing trip to Alaska, among other things."

JB described the strange events of the past week in Homer, including the murder of Richard Vandorn, the FBI's strange behavior, and the possible involvement of Senator Strunk.

"Wow. You probably want to know if I have any idea who might be behind the plot. I'm not surprised that Strunk may be involved. He has been associated with a cabal of intelligence operatives with sketchy motives."

"So, who among the feds can we trust? The FBI guys in Homer are acting like they are receiving orders from someone to treat Vandorn's murder like a secret national security incident, but at the same time, they seem clueless as to why."

"Can you create an encrypted file with the rest of the document and send it to me? I'll get back to you on a law enforcement strategy. I know you guys are going to keep investigating, so please be careful and keep me informed."

JB always felt wrung out after talking to Karl. His former trainer and supervisor symbolized the power structure during a difficult and unpleasant time in his life. But, at the same time, Karl was loyal and genuinely fond of JB. It was all very confusing—but now they needed each other.

———•———

Beverly awoke and wandered into the small living room. JB was sitting on the couch, staring into space. "So, what's up?"

"I just talked to Karl. He's going to try and find out who is responsible for Project Nemesis, and who in the agencies it might be safe to talk to."

"Does he think we're crazy?"

"He thinks someone is crazy, but I don't think it's us."

JB opened his phone and checked the tracking app to see John Melman's current location. Melman was on the move, currently driving on East End Road. Since Melman was away from his cabin, JB called the recording device and discovered that a phone conversation had occurred at eleven o'clock the previous night. The recorder picked up most of Melman's half of the conversation:

Hello

Yeah. There's some weird stuff going on in Homer. Some guy was killed on a fancy yacht in the harbor.

I don't know his name. A team of FBI agents has taken over the investigation from the local trooper, but they're not giving out any information. Even the local newspaper has been silent. Do you know what's going on?

Ok. I'll keep my eyes and ears open. If anything else happens, I'll let you know. So, what am I supposed to do now?

You know where I am. Let me know if you need anything.

"That wasn't very enlightening," said Beverly. "Who do you think was calling?"

"I guess the call could have come from anywhere," answered JB. "But, if we assume it originated in Alaska, then maybe the caller was the only other name we know, Stanley Krupp. It sounded like the caller was just trying to get a feel for the situation in Homer. One thing we did learn was that Melman wasn't involved in the murder. That probably would've been too easy. So, there's another violent person running around."

"If the Homer murder is, in fact, connected to Project Nemesis, we can probably assume that the conspirators, being political types, will make sure that they have deniability. They may have hired a professional assassin to do the dirty work, likely a former military person."

"If such a person does exist, maybe someone in town has seen him or her. We could ask people to look out for someone who doesn't fit in and looks ex-military," suggested JB. "We could talk to our old friend, Gertie."

Gertie was the proprietor of Gertie's Tavern, Homer's sleaziest bar. She was well known in Southcentral Alaska for her amazing physical attributes and the tattoos prominently displayed thereon, specifically an iguana plunging headfirst into Gertie's cleavage. While Gertie was a crude and bawdy woman, she was basically kindhearted and had helped out the Mooseketeers and the troopers on previous occasions.

CHAPTER 16

AT FIVE O'CLOCK MONDAY morning, JB and Charlie met downtown and picked up a trailer containing a Yamaha side-by-side four-wheeler. The ATV had space for two passengers and substantial gear. With each knobby wheel driving independently, the ubiquitous four-wheelers got amazing traction on a variety of terrain. Each of the passengers brought personal gear sufficient for overnight camping, if necessary. Of course, JB was equipped with his bag of spy tricks and his little Beretta handgun.

They drove out East End Road to its terminus, parked, and unloaded the ATV. A maze of trails headed north toward the Caribou Hills. Charlie had plotted a tentative route that he thought might get them within a mile and a half of Krupp's cabin. By seven o'clock, they were bouncing along through terrain that varied from upland spruce forest to muskeg. Their destination was about ten miles to the north as the crow flies, but the primitive trails did not follow a straight line, often bypassing soggy ground.

They crossed several streams, most of which were easily forded, but one small stream had such steep banks that the ATV got high-centered on the far side. The machine had a winch, but there were no trees in front of them for cable attachment. Fortunately, the owner of the ATV had anticipated such a situation and had included in the equipment box a stout stake that served as a portable tree. Charlie used a small sledge to pound the stake into the ground and attached the cable. Using a combination of winching and lifting, JB and Charlie managed to free the machine and continue on their way.

At two o'clock, they finally got to within a couple of miles of Krupp's cabin. They hid the ATV in dense brush and continued on foot. The terrain was very irregular. They crossed a series of parallel spruce-covered ridges alternating with bogs and small streams. Two hours and many expletives later, they crested a ridge and sighted the cabin. There was no plane by the airstrip and no smoke coming from the chimney. No one home.

Before leaving Homer, they had arranged to call Kate using JB's satellite phone to get the latest information on Krupp's whereabouts before approaching the cabin, hoping that the Facebook communications between Krupp and his daughter would provide insight. As far as Kate could tell, Stanley was probably on his way back to Alaska but not there yet. The Facebook postings suggested that Krupp could arrive sometime in late afternoon or evening.

"We'd better get going," said Charlie. "Obviously, if we hear a plane, we need to get the heck out of the cabin and out of sight."

"Yeah. The cabin door is on the side away from the airstrip, so we should be able to get out as the plane is landing. That will give us several minutes to hide. We should watch for cameras and other passive surveillance. Obviously, a standard security system would be useless out here, but Krupp might want to know if someone broke in while he was gone."

"Ok. Let's go."

JB and Charlie carefully approached the cabin door. While the exterior of the cabin consisted of raw logs and looked primitive, the door was high-quality with a commercial lock. JB went to work with his lock-picking kit.

"What's taking so long?" asked Charlie.

"Shut up. This is a challenging lock."

Finally, the lock clicked open. JB inspected the door for various intrusion indicators, such as a hair stuck to the door frame, but did not see anything suspicious. The two Mooseketeers entered slowly, looking for motion-activated alarms. While the exterior of the cabin appeared rugged, the interior was finished to the standards of an upscale subdivision. The inclusion of indoor plumbing was unusual in the Alaska bush. Furniture and kitchen appliances were high quality. JB could not help but compare Krupp's cabin with John Melman's squalid quarters. The two men obviously viewed life differently and had vastly different financial resources.

"The cabin is all electric, so presumably there is a generator in the shed out back," said Charlie.

"Yeah. Plus, it's set up for internet access with a satellite dish on the roof and cables to this little desk," replied JB as he looked through the desk drawers. "Unfortunately, there is no computer and nothing incriminating in the drawers."

"It appears that Mr. Krupp is one of Alaska's most sophisticated recluses. I guess that shouldn't surprise us, given his Ivy League background. We'd better get the listening device installed while we can."

"I'm on it," replied JB as he removed a light switch plate and squeezed the recorder into the space between the walls.

Additional search turned up nothing. Stanley Krupp was a very neat person. Even the waste baskets had been emptied.

"Do you hear a plane?" asked Charlie.

"Yep. Let's get the fuck out of here," answered JB as he ran for the door.

JB and Charlie quickly exited and sprinted toward a clump of bushes on the edge of the lake. They heard sounds of a plane taxiing, and a few minutes later, a man, presumably Stanley Krupp, walked around the side of the cabin and entered the front door. Immediately, the generator started, and a light went on in the cabin.

"This may be a lucky break," said JB. "We may be able to hear something from here."

"That assumes Krupp doesn't figure out his sanctuary has been compromised. I noticed a gun safe, so he probably has substantial firepower."

"Always the pessimist."

"It's starting to get dark. We need to find a safe place to camp for the night."

JB and Charlie carefully moved out of sight of the cabin and found a sheltered spot on the other side of a narrow ridge to pitch a small tent. After preparing for the night, they wandered back in the moonlight to within sight of the cabin. At about nine o'clock, the cabin lights went out—apparently, Stanley was not a night owl.

———◆———

CHARLIE STIRRED IN HIS sleeping bag as the light seeped into the tent from the rising sun. He moved over, expecting to cuddle with Kate, but was stopped by the confines of the mummy bag. Opening his eyes, he was momentarily startled as he gazed into the face of JB, who was still snoring in his own bag just a few inches away. Yikes! Charlie thought there were better ways to wake up when he heard the sound of an airplane warming up. He punched JB, eliciting various annoyed noises from inside the sleeping bag.

"What the heck is going on?" JB mumbled.

"Krupp is leaving already," said Charlie as the sound of the plane increased and the plane obviously accelerated and lifted off.

"I wonder what he's doing up so early."

"I don't know, but it may give us another opportunity to look around."

"This might be a good time to test whether my recorder is working," said JB as he turned on his satellite phone while still in his sleeping bag. Putting the phone on speaker, he called the listening device in the cabin and entered the code to play any recordings made overnight. They could hear the sound-activated recorder turning on and off in response to various sounds within the cabin—dishes clinking in the sink and a chair being pushed back from a table. Then the sound of a mobile phone ringing was followed by a one-sided conversation:

What's up, Senator?

Yeah, I heard that Vandorn was killed in Homer. What the fuck was he doing here?

How did he get wind of our plans?

As far as I know, the FBI took over the investigation from Alaska authorities, but I don't know any more than that.

Are you going to be able to control the investigation?

Ok, I'll take your word for it.

I collected some information for the first phase of our plans. It should be workable.

Yeah, the meeting here is still on for July 15. As far as I know everyone has finalized their plans.

I'll see you then.

"Well, that was pretty interesting," said Charlie. "It looks like your spy toys are going to be very helpful once again."

"Knowing that there's going to be a meeting on July 15 is hugely important. With some luck, we might be able to determine the identity of all the conspirators," added JB.

"If you can manage to get out of your sleeping bag, we should take another look around before Krupp gets back."

After packing up their minimal campsite and returning the area to more or less original condition, the intrepid duo trekked back to the cabin and peered in the windows.

"Do you see a computer or a briefcase?" asked Charlie.

"No. I can see the desktop and, there is nothing there. It may not be worth breaking in again if there is nothing new to see."

"I agree," said Charlie as he looked in the bedroom window. "There is an open duffel bag on the bed, so Krupp is probably coming back today. I don't see any documents or written materials. Let's take a quick look at the generator shed and then head back home."

Like the cabin, the primitive exterior of the generator shed belied the quality of its contents. The walls and ceiling were lined with thick sound-deadening insulation. The generator was a new commercial diesel model, more than adequate to provide all the power needs of Stanley Krupp. A small workbench was built into one wall with the tools necessary for generator maintenance on a pegboard above the bench.

"I think we're done here. Is there anything else you want to see?" asked Charlie.

"No. Let's head back. Maybe we can get home in time for dinner."

JB and Charlie retraced their path from the day before—back to the ATV, then to their vehicle at the end of East End Road, and finally back to Beverly's cabin, where Kate and Beverly eagerly awaited news of their adventure.

Chapter 17

While Charlie and JB were *en route* back to Homer, Karl, JB's old boss, was comfortably seated on his oversized recliner in front of a roaring fire in the huge rock fireplace in his home in Arlington, Virginia. Karl was seventy-five years old and had the appearance of a university professor. He was slender and of average height with abundant brown hair, metal-rimmed glasses, and a pale complexion. It was not at all obvious that he had once been a Navy SEAL, a characteristic that often caused other people to underestimate his tenacity. He finished reading the Project Nemesis document and sat back with a serious frown. Karl was supposedly retired from government intelligence work, but no one actually retired from such a position. He was seriously conflicted. How should he handle the information given to him by JB?

During his forty years of clandestine service for the government, he had been involved in various activities that might be considered outside the legitimate authority of the U.S. Government. Nevertheless, this conspiracy was beyond the pale. On one hand, it seemed ridiculous that a couple of civilians in Homer, Alaska, would be the primary bulwark against such an insane idea as systematic assassination to mold the government power structure. But he was at a loss to come up with a better idea. Political infighting, insider intrigue, and massive egos made it difficult to navigate the complexities of Washington—or to separate the good guys from the bad guys.

Karl needed to do some investigating, but the danger of accidentally contacting someone who was a member of the conspiracy was real. He started calling contacts in the FBI and CIA that he was confidant would not be involved in the conspiracy. His initial questions were vague, asking whether there were rumors of rogue agents or politicians with agendas of their own. But no one had any ideas. His last call was to a member of his old team—the team that had originally included JB. "Ethan" suggested that there might be something going on well beyond the normal political dirty tricks. The word on the street was that a group of rogue members of the congressional power structure and the intelligence community was coalescing into a potentially dangerous cabal. At least one person from the FBI was supposedly involved.

Karl sent a brief text to JB outlining his findings and warning of FBI contacts.

———◆———

CHARLIE AND JB MANAGED to get back to Homer by five o'clock. They were dirty, smelly, and exhausted from lack of sleep. Their butts were sore from continual pounding as the ATV jounced along the muddy trail. After returning the four-wheeler to Charlie's friend and getting cleaned up, they met with Kate and Beverly at Mama's Fish House. Also invited to dinner was Michael Vandorn, who had returned to Homer that afternoon. Charlie and JB recounted the highlights of their sneaky excursion.

"How did everything go in San Juan?" Kate asked Michael.

"I guess about as well as a memorial service can go," answered Michael. "There was nobody there from Washington, D.C., which was just as well since the Vandorn family friends are not very fond of Senator Strunk. No one could understand why Richard went to work for him in the first place, and there was much discussion about what the senator may have been involved in. But, all in all, it was good that some of our old friends got together."

"Did anybody have any ideas about the senator's activities?" asked JB.

"A lot of suspicion but no ideas," replied Michael.

"OK. So, what do we do now?" asked Beverly as a pitcher of beer was delivered to the table.

"Well, we know that there is going to be a meeting at Krupp's cabin on July 15, so eavesdropping on that meeting should be a top priority," said Charlie as he poured beer. "Obviously, we will continue listening to our bugs at Melman's and Krupp's cabins and track Melman's car movements."

Conversation stopped as a waitress arrived with platters of deep-fried beer-battered halibut and mountains of fries.

"Maybe Beverly and I should plan on watching Krupp's cabin during the meeting," said JB.

"What, you're going to pass up another opportunity for my company?" quipped Charlie.

"Actually, I was thinking that Beverly's photographic experience would be valuable, not to mention her expensive long lens camera," said JB. "Also, waking up next to your face again in a tiny tent is a scary prospect."

"What will you be trying to find out at Krupp's?" Michael asked.

"I was thinking that a main goal would be simply to identify the conspiracy members by observing and photographing as they get off the plane," said JB. "Krupp's plane can only carry two or three people at a time, so presumably he will be making several trips."

"If we get good enough photos, we'll probably be able to utilize facial recognition software to identify at least some of the participants," added Kate. "As it happens, my brother just sent me a program that he's been using."

"We can also listen to what's going on in the cabin in real time, assuming that the recorder can isolate individual conversations," added Beverly. "That will give us something to do while we are wait-ing for plane loads of bad guys."

"Michael, what are your plans?" asked Charlie.

"I'm gonna make myself comfortable on Richard's boat first of all, including learning how to operate it. Then I'll probably talk to the trooper to see what kind of progress they're making on the murder investigation. Maybe I can learn something about what happened to the FBI, who have apparently left the area."

"Since I've been rudely kicked off the Krupp cabin surveillance team, I should be free to help out with boat stuff," added Charlie.

Small talk dominated the conversation for the rest of the meal, and the tired participants dispersed to their respective habitats for the night.

CHAPTER 18

MIDMORNING THE FOLLOWING DAY, Dick Whelan, the mystery man from Richard Vandorn's notebook, stuck his hand out of the window of his motel room on the outskirts of Homer. He was attempting to smoke a cigarette without getting any smoke in the room, but was only marginally successful. It was bad enough he had to spend most of his time hidden in his crappy room, but cutting back on cigarettes was a step too far. It wasn't right that an accomplished person such as himself was being treated so poorly. Unfortunately, hiding out was an occupational hazard in his chosen profession. He had been told by his most recent employers to remain on standby in Homer and await his next assignment.

Whelan was ex-military Special Forces. He was of average height and weight with short brown hair and a narrow face with no obvious distinguishing features. Various manly tattoos covered his arms; consequently, he tended to wear long-sleeve shirts to hide the obvious identifying features. He had monetized his skill set by hiring himself out to perform various acts of violence for anyone with money.

He suspected that the people who hired him this time considered themselves to be bastions of the moral high ground, but Dick knew that it was all bullshit. They just wanted more money and more power. His instructions were always delivered anonymously. Nevertheless, he had traced the texts to Washington, D.C. and strongly suspected that

government officials were involved. Not that it made any difference—
he just liked to know with whom he was dealing. The last message
suggested that there would be a challenging and lucrative assignment
in the near future. Inquiries into his skill as a sniper hinted at assassination—that was alright with him as long as the setup was reasonably
safe. He had insisted on checking things out before the act so that he
could analyze the potential danger.

As Whelan reclined on his uncomfortable bed, feeling sorry for
himself, a new encrypted text came in on one of his burner phones.
The decoded message suggested that he set aside the time period
encompassed by the first week of August. It also suggested that he
acquire a rifle suitable for accurate fire at a distance of at least several
hundred feet. He seldom traveled with any weapons, because it was
just too risky. Acquiring guns on site usually involved less risk, especially in a place like Alaska, where guns were everywhere and could be
purchased privately without any record.

After thinking about the gun situation, Whelan decided that it
would be safer and more anonymous to buy a rifle in Anchorage,
where there were many gun stores, some of which were less than dili-
gent at checking identification. Although Anchorage was an annoying
four-hour drive, hiding out in Homer made him crazy. He decided to
leave immediately so that he could reward himself with a night on the
town and maybe female accompaniment.

Whelan arrived in Anchorage in late afternoon and went directly to
a sketchy gun shop in a rundown strip mall on the south side of town.
Before entering the store, he donned fake glasses and a COVID mask.
He told the proprietor that he was looking for a used big game rifle in
a .308 caliber with a high-quality scope. It just happened that there was
a suitable gun on the store's rack of used rifles. He purchased the gun
using cash and his current fake ID. An extra fifty dollars assured that the
serial number would be inadvertently left off the purchase documents.

"So, what's with the mask?" asked the proprietor. "No one in
Anchorage wears masks."

"I recently had a liver transplant and need to be super careful about infections," answered Whelan.

"I guess that makes sense. Take care and enjoy the rifle."

After a comfortable night at a nice hotel, accompanied temporarily by an attractive and expensive young hooker, Whelan left early and drove to a shooting range that he had passed on the way into town. Since it was on his way and likely to be uncrowded on a weekday morning, he decided it was as good a time as any to test his new acquisition. The range was manned by a sleepy state employee who barely looked at him as he checked in and bought a couple of targets. He proceeded to sight in the rifle at one hundred yards, the longest-range distance. He was pleased with the rifle's performance. Only a few minor scope adjustments were required to consistently hit near the bullseye. He experimented with different settings to try and predict what changes might need to be made under varying distances and wind conditions. It was not perfect, but good enough for his purposes.

———•———

Meanwhile, Stanley Krupp lounged on his plush couch, reading a Tom Clancy novel. He had decided to stay in Alaska until the team meeting scheduled for the following week. The day before, he had dealt with some of his various business interests in Southcentral Alaska, mostly associated with sport fishing on the Kenai River. He met with the manager of a fishing lodge in which he had a partial interest and had beers with several guides. They were excited about the planned visit by the vice president to their favorite river, which was to occur in about three weeks. No one knew exactly where he would be fishing or who had been contracted to guide him, but the general consensus was that the publicity could only help their business.

When not in Kenai with his drinking buddies, Stanley hung out at his cabin, flying in and out as needed. He stayed busy maintaining his plane and cabin and coordinating various aspects of Project

Nemesis. He prepared a detailed description of his plans for the VP assassination, including directions to the sniper nest, and sent them in encrypted emails to Dick Whelan. He also mailed the GPS mapping device he had used during his reconnaissance that contained the exact location and route to the nest. He recommended that Whelan very carefully conduct a dry run in the near future. Stanley Krupp had not met Whelan and did not intend to meet him. Communications were via text on burner phones and a P.O. Box in Homer. It was almost certain that Whelan was not his real name. The assassin did not know where the instructions came from and did not want to know.

Chapter 19

The next few days passed with reasonable normality. Kate labored at FlashFrozen, Beverly marketed her private investigation business, Charlie kept up with correspondence relating to his ecotour business, and JB pretended he was busy working on his book. No new information came from the listening devices in Krupp's and Melman's cabins. The tracker on John Melman's Blazer indicated a pattern of movement from his cabin to Gertie's Tavern and back again. Not very enlightening.

Meanwhile, Michael Vandorn set up housekeeping on the Wonky and passed the time by reading the multitude of instruction manuals for all the mechanical systems and navigational instruments. He took a few practice runs out into the bay to get used to the boat and practice solo docking. He liked the boat and enjoyed the challenge. Nights were a little nerve-racking. He did not know whether he was now a target of the man who had killed his brother, so he jury-rigged an intrusion alarm by stringing monofilament fishing line around the perimeter of the boat connected to various noisy kitchen utensils. He continued to sleep with a gun under his pillow.

When it was evening in Washington, D.C., Michael called Richard's former secretary, Phyllis. He discovered that she had been laid off by Senator Strunk as soon as Richard's death was discovered. She was obviously not a big fan of the senator.

"Do you have any idea why Richard drove his boat to Alaska?" asked Michael.

"No, he didn't mention a boat trip to me. But his decision to take time off from the Senator's office was a surprise. He changed his originally scheduled vacation time without specifying a reason," replied Phyllis.

"What was his state of mind?"

"He was clearly agitated about something, presumably something that the Senator had said or done, but I don't know specifically what it was. I do know that Senator Strunk had been on a rampage the day before. His rants were sort of nonspecific—complaining about the government as a whole being totally worthless. Michael got up and left during the tantrum and didn't come back."

"OK. That's interesting. Did the senator mention Alaska or any names?"

"He didn't mention Alaska or any particular names, but, as always, he was disgusted with anything going on in Congress. I think he called them lily-livered losers."

"Thanks for the information, Phyllis. It might be a good idea if you took extra precautions to keep yourself safe. I don't think you're in danger, but there's too much weird stuff going on."

"I pretty much already figured that out. I'm planning on visiting friends for a while, especially since I'm currently unemployed."

"Goodbye and take care."

———◆———

DICK WHELAN AROSE EARLY on the same day, drove north to the Sterling Highway and headed east to the side road indicated by the navigation device given to him by his anonymous contact. He parked his rental car out of sight and walked into the woods near the spot shown on his instructions. As he continued to trace Stanley's route to the proposed sniper nest on the Kenai River, Whelan thought back to his military experiences. He had encountered difficult overland travel routes during his training and during deployment, but nothing quite like this. In some ways, it was worse than the jungle, with fallen trees at all different angles and devil's club shrubs with nasty thorns. As he was pushing himself through a dense patch, he stepped on a devil's club branch, which snapped back between his legs, penetrating his jeans and impaling sensitive areas. Fuck!

The hiking became easier as he reached higher ground adjacent to the riverbank. But as he got close to the river's edge, he was forced onto his hands and knees so he could crawl under the spruce saplings. It was so dense that he almost crawled over the edge of the bank. The cleared nest was right where it was supposed to be, marked by red flagging tape. Whelan settled into the spot selected by his unknown predecessor and observed the river. Although the site was hard to get to, he basically approved of the location. It was well hidden from all sides and above and provided clear sight lines to the river and any boat that happened to be drifting past.

Whelan had not brought his new rifle to avoid the possibility of having to answer questions should he meet someone, but he had brought a range finder. He checked the distance to near and far banks and estimated the likely distance to a boat in the middle of the channel. He also estimated the vertical drop from his position to the river. It all seemed doable. It would not be an especially long shot, and he was not too worried about the more technical aspects of extreme long-distance shooting.

The next thing Whelan analyzed was the chance of escape from his riverbank position. He had not been told the name of the target, but it was a safe assumption that it was someone important. Consequently, there would very likely be security precautions. He did not know whether such precautions might include a boat accompanying the target boat or maybe even overhead reconnaissance via drone. Regardless, he would need to get out of there quickly. But roadblocks on the limited highway system would be a certainty and could be set up before he would have a chance to leave the area. Whelan began to think about hiding somewhere nearby until the coast was clear. He could hide out in the woods for a couple of days, but a serious search might involve helicopters with infrared sensing or tracking dogs, either of which might uncover his position. Alternatively, he could hide out in one of the many seasonal cabins along the river. But nearby cabins would be an obvious place to search.

Whelan needed to think carefully about the escape situation. He timed the hike back to his car and concluded it would take too long. Authorities would have plenty of time to establish roadblocks and search efforts. They might even find his car before he could get to it. He needed to think outside the box, but was having trouble coming up with any ideas.

Chapter 20

On July fourteenth, JB and Beverly repeated the long, uncomfortable trip to Krupp's cabin without much difficulty, reaching the area by mid-afternoon. They tried to maintain a screen of vegetation between themselves and the cabin for the last half mile to eliminate the possibility of being seen. But when they got within sight of the cabin, they could see that there was no plane on the airstrip.

"Since no one's here, let's check out the recon site Charlie and I picked out. See what you think," suggested JB.

"Roger that," answered Beverly.

They skirted the property around to the ridge top with a view of the cabin and airstrip. "Is this close enough to identify faces from photos with your long lens?" asked JB.

Beverly attached the thousand-millimeter lens to her camera and viewed the area at the end of the airstrip where passengers would presumably be disembarking. She snapped a couple of shots of a tree at the edge of the plane parking area and looked at the little digital image on the back of her Nikon. She zoomed in and looked at the texture of the bark.

"I think this will work when enlarged on a computer. The resolution looks pretty good. My brother just sent me some facial recognition software, which I think will be able to match at least some of the faces with persons in available databases, especially since most of these people are probably government employees."

"We may recognize some of the faces ourselves," said JB.

"Crap, I hope not. That would mean the conspirators are high enough officials to get their photos on TV or in the papers. That wouldn't give me much confidence in our elected officials."

They reclined on the comfortable, spongy ground and watched the cabin. The late afternoon sun was warm, and the wind was still. Small birds flitted around them, picking at the moss for goodies to eat. A loon called from the nearby lake, and the flute-like call of thrushes emanated from unseen locations.

"We better set up camp while it's still light. If Krupp arrives, we should be able to hear his plane in time to hustle back here," suggested JB as he unfolded his lanky body from the ground.

JB led the way to the same hidden camping spot used before by him and Charlie. They set up the small camouflaged tent and laid out their sleeping bags.

"Do you hear a plane?" asked Beverly.

"Yeah. Let's get back up there. Krupp may have someone with him."

The duo reached their observation post a few minutes later, just in time to see the plane taxi back from the end of the landing strip. Beverly pulled a pair of ten-power image-stabilized binoculars from her pack and watched as the plane shut down. After Beverly had received her private investigator license, she applied for a bank loan and bought some tools of the trade, including the binoculars and the expensive camera. The items were proving to be very useful.

"It looks like Krupp is alone," said Beverly. They watched as Stanley Krupp carried a briefcase and a duffel bag to the front door, entered the cabin, and fired up the generator. Soon, smoke was coming from the chimney.

A cold breeze began to blow down from the mountains, accompanied by a light drizzle. "There's not much more we can do here. Let's get the photographic equipment out of the rain," said Beverly as the two spies moved away from the cabin, over the ridge, and into their tent under the trees.

"So, what do we do now?" asked JB.

"I don't know. But I may have some ideas," said Beverly as she scooched into their double sleeping bag. "Are spies allowed to make love while on duty?"

"I'll have to consult my spy manual."

———◆———

Beverly awoke early as the sun illuminated their tent, sunrise occurring at about five o'clock on the Kenai Peninsula in mid-July. She lay there a while listening to the birds. The loon on the lake seemed to be having some sort of meltdown. She heard crunching nearby and stuck her head out of the tent. A moose was casually munching on willows about fifty feet from their tent. It was a sleek young bull with velvet-covered antlers. Having grown up in Los Angeles, Beverly was fascinated by the ungainly animals and had recently read an article on moose behavior. Scientists who study the animals had been speculating for decades regarding the adaptive function of seemingly impractical decorations such as antlers. Why would an animal carry sixty pounds of unnecessary weight on the top of its head? Plus, big antlers get in the way when walking through dense woods. Every year, bull moose get tangled in swing sets and jungle gyms in Anchorage. While competing bulls sometimes joust during the rut, the article suggested that simple sex appeal is the main evolutionary driving force. Big antlers on the horny bulls impress the cows and lead to more mating success. Beverly contemplated the parallels to human beings.

Unable to wait any longer, Beverly got up to pee and emerged into the early morning. The moose nonchalantly wandered out of sight, seemingly having no interest in the two-legged intruder. Mist hung over the lowest parts of the valley, but the sky above was clear, and it looked like it was going to be a nice day.

Beverly started a pot of coffee on the little camp stove to avoid any visible smoke. Amazingly, JB emerged from the tent just as the coffee was ready. After eating a field breakfast of stale pastries and fruit, the dynamic duo disassembled their little camp and stashed the camping gear to get it out of sight of the activity that was expected to occur later in the day.

They hiked to their observation post overlooking Krupp's cabin. They anticipated spending most of the day in their comfortable nest hidden from view. They covered themselves with military-type camouflage netting to minimize being seen from above. At six-thirty, the cabin generator turned on, signaling that Krupp was awake. At seven-fifteen, Krupp left the cabin, walked to his plane, and took off, banking away from the Mooseketeer's observation post.

"Since Stanley will probably be gone for at least an hour, let's see if he talked on the phone last night," suggested JB as he removed the satellite phone from his goody pack. JB and Beverly listened as the recorder hidden in the cabin played back any sounds from the previous night. There were the usual sounds of Stanley preparing some dinner and moving around the cabin. Then, at nine o'clock, Stanley's phone rang:

This is Krupp

Yeah, Mack. Plans are still on for tomorrow. Meet at the designated place at eight o'clock.

I'll be making either two or three trips, depending on luggage and weight. So, everyone should be here by lunchtime. See you then.

"Well, that wasn't very enlightening, but at least we know we haven't wasted three days," said Beverly as she mounted her camera on a short tripod and adjusted the exposure settings.

While waiting for Krupp to return, the couple reclined on the soft mossy ground and relaxed, looking up at fluffy white clouds. Chickadees flitted around them, probing at bark crevices, and juncos hopped on the ground, picking at bugs. The nearby loon continued its eerie lament, punctuated by demonic-sounding warbled cries.

"I hear the plane," said JB. "Get ready."

The Cessna circled, landed at the far end of the strip, and taxied back toward the cabin. Beverly took a couple of photos of the plane, then lined up her view on the door. Four passengers disembarked, including Krupp. Beverly photographed each passenger as they exited the plane and again when they walked around to the front door of the cabin. Meanwhile, JB looked through the binoculars, trying to memorize faces.

"Holy shit," exclaimed JB. "One of those guys is the Defense Secretary, Mack Fraser. One of the other guys looks familiar, but I can't come up with a name."

"Wow. I guess the conspiracy does go to the highest level. How are we supposed to deal with someone like Fraser?"

"I think we let other people handle the high-level folks. Probably the best we can do is try to minimize damage in Alaska."

Stanley Krupp returned to his plane and took off for the next load. His passengers entered the cabin, brought coffee out onto the front porch, and sat looking at the lake.

"Will your directional microphone pick up voices from this distance? Obviously, the cabin listening device doesn't do us much good if they're outside."

"I'm not sure, but let's try it," answered JB.

The parabolic microphone, designed primarily for birdwatchers, had an advertised range of up to three hundred feet. He plugged the microphone into its amplifier/recorder and put on headphones.

"I can just barely hear them. Maybe if I adjust the gain and volume, it will work better. OK, I think we're in business. Right now, they're just bullshitting—talking about fishing and other macho stuff."

"Let me know if they say anything significant."

JB and Beverly continued to observe and listen to the gaggle of manly men lounging on the cabin porch. Their exploits as amazing outdoorsmen dominated the conversation.

Thirty minutes after Krupp's departure, the plane returned with another load of apparent conspirators. This time, five people emerged from the plane and made their way to the cabin.

"Since the Cessna only has seats for four people, one of those guys must have been crammed into the baggage compartment. I wonder how they chose which person would go as a suitcase," quipped JB.

As before, Beverly photographed each man as he disembarked and again at the cabin door. JB peered through binoculars. The new group obtained drinks from the cabin and assembled with the others on the cabin porch, all seated around a large picnic-type table. Stanley Krupp sat at one end, and Defense Secretary Mack Fraser at the other end.

"I don't recognize any of these other guys. Maybe if I watched more cable TV, I'd be better informed," said JB.

"I don't recognize any of them either. I guess we can assume by the seating positions at the table that Krupp and Fraser are the leaders."

———◆———

"OK, WE'RE ALL HERE, and it's a beautiful day to discuss the changes that we would like to make to our dysfunctional governmental leadership," said Mack Fraser as he stood at the head of the table. "Stan, why don't you give us a rundown on the progress of our first phase?"

"Things are falling into place for the removal of the Vice President. Thanks to his staff's indiscretion, I've determined Taylor's travel schedule and arrangements for fishing excursions. He'll arrive in Alaska on August 5 and fish on the Kenai River the next day. I've explored and picked out a potential sniper location along the river and hired a reliable person to do the sniping. Nobody knows his real name, including me. All arrangements have been remote and anonymous. At my insistence, our sniper has personally scoped out the site and agrees that it is viable and secure, at least until the shot is fired.

"The biggest problem our sniper faces is getting away after the deed is accomplished. Because of security around the vice president, the area will be cordoned off immediately after the vice president is shot. There is only one highway out of the area. Our guy is concerned, but thinks he will be able to get away. In any event, he doesn't have information on any of us. If he is caught, it shouldn't affect us or our plans for the future."

"So, what does happen after Taylor is deceased?" asked Greg Dixon, Deputy Secretary of Homeland Security.

"The procedure as set forth in the twenty-fifth amendment calls for the president to nominate someone for the position, followed by confirmation of both houses of Congress," answered Mack Fraser. "Our plan is for President Evans to nominate me for the position."

"How do we know that he is going to do that?" asked John Frisch, chief legal counsel for the CIA. "As far as I know, President Evans isn't all that fond of you."

"That's true, but we have significant dirt on the president, some of which is pretty embarrassing," answered Fraser. "We're confident that he'll be compliant."

"OK. And then what? What is the next step?" inquired Frisch.

"That's one of the things we need to discuss at this meeting," replied Stanley Krupp as he passed out pastries and coffee. "Greg's boss, the Homeland Security Secretary, has been a thorn in the side of those of us who would like to take a tougher stance on a number of issues."

"I'll second that," said Greg Dixon. "Besides, she's a bitch."

"We should probably keep personal animosity out of this as much as possible, but I agree that Gloria Alvarez should be removed," added Mack Fraser. "All in favor, raise your hands."

Everyone raised their hand except Joel Levine, an FBI lawyer.

"I assume by 'remove' you are suggesting permanent removal from the planet. There must be a less drastic alternative. How about manufacturing a job-killing scandal?"

"I think that's worth thinking about. The death of a female cabinet secretary might invite close scrutiny," suggested Mack Fraser. "Let's wait and see what happens after Taylor is out of the way."

"Speaking of death, what's the deal with the murder of Senator Strunk's Chief of Staff?" asked Levine. "Did you guys have anything to do with that?"

"That wasn't part of our plan," said Krupp. "Although the senator is part of our group, he may have been acting on his own."

"Where is the senator?" asked Levine.

"He wasn't able to break away for this meeting," replied Mack Fraser. "I suspect, as usual, he is trying to preserve deniability."

"One thing that concerns me is the fact that Richard Vandorn's brother is a federal prosecutor and has been nosing around," said Levine. "He may be smart enough to figure out that something is going on."

"Yeah. We'll need to keep track of that. I have assigned one of our more supportive citizens in Homer to sniff around," replied Stanley. "Hopefully, Vandorn has been preoccupied with putting his brother's remains in the ground."

The rest of the meeting was dedicated to a discussion of the kinds of changes that a new regime might enact. The overall goals of the group remained somewhat vague, exacerbated by the fact that the members were not all on the same page. As coffee drinking changed to beer drinking, the conversations became more heated. By late afternoon, the contingent advocating military takeover of the executive branch, led by Fraser, was yelling at the contingent advocating for a more subtle form of insurrection.

Stanley Krupp, as the designated flyer, had not been drinking and tried to calm things down. At four o'clock, he loaded the hawkish contingent into the plane and returned them to their vehicles in Soldotna. The peaceable group returned in the second trip. Stanley hoped they would stay away from each other during the remainder of their stay in Alaska.

CHAPTER 21

"HOLY SHIT," SAID BEVERLY when JB played the recording of the conversation about killing the vice president. "We're sitting on some very dangerous information. What the hell do we do with it?"

After Krupp left with the second load of whackos, JB and Beverly sanitized their observation post and retreated to their campsite. Beverly used the smart satphone to send photos and recordings of the rebel group to Charlie and suggested that he call them to discuss next steps. Ten minutes later, Charlie called.

"Wow," said Charlie. "We've stumbled on a hornet's nest. Obviously, we are in way over our heads. We need to get this information to high-level people we can trust as soon as possible to head off the assassination and put things in motion to stop these guys. I recommend that we see if Michael Vandorn can work through his justice department buddies to pass the word. Preferably all the way up to the president."

"I agree," said JB. "I can also talk to Karl, my contact in Washington. Maybe he can work with Vandorn to come up with a plan for breaking up the conspiracy."

"It's too late for us to head back to Homer tonight, but we can be there by tomorrow afternoon," added Beverly. "Maybe Kate can start running the images through her facial recognition program before we get back. Did you recognize any of those guys, Charlie?"

"No, but I haven't had a chance to look at them on the computer yet. I can show them to Vandorn before you get back. He's closer to people in power and may know some of them. Be careful on your way back. I'll see you tomorrow."

After disconnecting with Charlie, JB and Beverly sat on a log at their minimal campsite. Beverly had surreptitiously slipped two cans of beer into her pack before leaving Homer and broke them out to celebrate a successful day of spying.

"Wow, what did I do to deserve such a thoughtful and crazy girl-friend?" asked Charlie as he popped the top on one of the cans.

"As long as you don't forget you owe me big time."

"I can probably pay you back later in the tent."

"You obviously have a high opinion of your skills as a lover."

As the sun descended toward the southeastern horizon, the air temperature cooled, and mosquitoes swarmed the camp. The two spies retreated to their tent. The loons resumed their insane dialogue at the lake, and other night birds began their haunting nocturnal calls.

Night sounds could also be heard coming from inside the tent.

———◆———

CHARLIE AND KATE CAREFULLY reviewed the amazing data dump sent by JB and Beverly. After finishing, they each poured themselves a glass of wine and sat in thoughtful silence.

"We should call Michael Vandorn," Charlie said after a few minutes.

"Yeah," added Kate. "Do we still need to avoid being seen together?"

"I guess. I haven't seen any FBI guys around, but whoever killed Richard Vandorn may still be here and keeping track of things. Our boat is too easy to surveil—someone could just sit above the harbor and see who comes and goes."

"Maybe we could meet at Beverly's cabin. I have the key since we work together. Also, we could take a first shot at facial recognition with the program on Beverly's big computer."

Michael answered on the first ring. They agreed to meet in an hour, driving separately and staggering their arrival times.

Kate and Charlie arrived first, and a few minutes later let Michael Vandorn into Beverly's cozy cabin. Kate transferred the images and recordings from her phone to Beverly's computer. They all reviewed the enlarged photos.

"I recognize some of these guys," Michael said, pointing at the screen. "That's Mack Fraser, Defense Secretary, and the guy in the middle of the table is a top lawyer for the CIA, John Frisch. Some of the other faces seem familiar, but I don't have their names."

Kate played the recording of the discussion centered on getting rid of the vice president.

"Crap," said Michael. "I can't believe these guys are for real. We definitely need to get word to somebody who can actually do something. It sounds like we might not even be able to count on the president."

"On the other hand, if the president is worried about a scandal, he may want to head off the plot before it gets out of hand," suggested Charlie. "We really don't know how he would react."

Meanwhile, Kate fiddled with the Otterly Ridiculous Investigations computer, loading one of the images from the secret meeting into the facial recognition program. The powerful computer began cranking away. "I've never used this program before, so I don't know how well it's going to work."

"So, for right now, I guess we wait for JB and Beverly to get back and then come up with a plan of action," Charlie said as he watched the computer compare hundreds of faces in a continuous blur. "It's too late to do anything else tonight."

"I'll make some calls first thing in the morning to selected colleagues at the Justice Department in Seattle," said Michael as he put on his coat. "I have some ideas for getting attention in Washington. See you guys tomorrow."

Chapter 22

"THE EXCREMENT IS STARTING to hit the fan," remarked Michael Vandorn. "This morning, I started the process of notifying selected people about the threats from Project Nemesis. I sent the audio and video from your surveillance to my boss in Seattle. He was obviously very disturbed, and we discussed who in D.C. to notify. The vice president's chief of staff is a former federal prosecutor from our district, and we both trust him, so he was sent an encrypted copy. He, in turn, showed it to the VP. They were both concerned about the trustworthiness of the VP's secret service detail, but agreed that the head of the detail, who has been with Taylor for many years, needed to be involved. So, that's where it stands so far."

The four Mooseketeers plus Vandorn were sitting in Beverly's living room. Cups of coffee and cookies adorned the rustic coffee table between them.

The two resident spies had mostly recovered from their long, bumpy ride back from Krupp's cabin, but their weariness was evident, compounded by two nights of sleeping on the ground and the stress of knowing stuff they really didn't want to know. A few steps away, in Beverly's office, the facial recognition program on the Otterly Ridiculous Investigations' computer continued to crank away as one face after another scrolled across the screen.

"Is the VP going to cancel his trip?" asked Kate between bites on a cinnamon roll.

"We talked about that," replied Vandorn. "The VP and his Chief of Staff suggested that we go through with the trip to flush out the sniper and demonstrate that a conspiracy exists. The problem is figuring out how to do that without anyone getting killed. It could be hard to find a volunteer to take Taylor's place in the fishing boat. You guys have any ideas?"

"A very realistic manikin or humanoid robot comes to mind," suggested Charlie. "Except it's pretty hard to make a fake person look natural, especially if the sniper has an opportunity to observe the boat long enough to see whether the occupants are acting normally."

"Could a human target be protected with armor?" asked Kate.

"A sniper round will penetrate most body armor, plus the head and other parts of the body would still be exposed," said JB.

"OK, no real human targets," Beverly said as she refilled coffee cups. "All we need is a totally realistic robot capable of holding and casting a fishing rod. Does such a thing exist?"

"I guess we could try and find out, but we don't have much time," added Vandorn.

"The other alternative is to find the sniper before he does his thing, but, given the amount of wild country, that seems like a difficult task," said Charlie. "I guess drones with heat-sensing equipment could fly over the fishing route, but a smart sniper will likely guard against routine aerial surveillance, since normal security for the VP will probably employ aerial surveillance regardless of whether a known threat exists. Insulated blankets can probably defeat the infrared sensor. Also, there are a lot of large, warm-blooded animals out there."

"The secret service guy told me that they planned to have two boats with the VP in one of them, probably the first boat," said Vandorn. "Theoretically, if a shot is taken, the boats could immediately go to shore with some of the agents chasing the sniper overland. Drones or helicopters could attempt to flush out the sniper from above. Presumably, the sniper will be expecting that reaction and will have prepared for it. How might the gunman protect himself under those circumstances, which are likely to occur, whether the VP is actually in the boat or not?"

"I've been thinking about that," added JB as he grabbed a third cookie. "The first thing we need to do is try to guess the most likely locations for the sniper nest. Michael, do we have details on the river locations where the fishing will happen and the kinds of boats that will be used?"

"Taylor's chief of staff is going to send me the details, but apparently there will be two excursions on August 6—a morning trip on the lower Kenai River in a continuously powered boat for chinook salmon, and an afternoon trip on the upper river where the boats will power upstream and then drift back down while fishing along the way for salmon and trout."

"We should be able to narrow things down quite a bit," said Charlie. "The lower river is busy and heavily populated with cabins, while the upper river has long, undeveloped stretches. Also, drift fishing on the upper river would provide a much easier target for the sniper. Plus, we need to consider the side of the river that is most advantageous to the gunman. Terrain south of the upper river is mostly wilderness for many miles. A gunman would have to cross the river to get there, and cross the river again to get to a transportation corridor."

"Given the danger and difficulty of providing a decoy for the sniper to shoot at," contributed JB, "it may be worthwhile trying to find the sniper nest before Taylor gets here. We know that at least two people, Krupp and the sniper, have hiked to a prospective site. So, it may be possible to find their trail and locate the sniper nest."

"Isn't that like looking for a needle in a haystack?" Kate asked.

"Yeah, but I think we have enough information that it's worth a try," JB replied.

"We know from our past adventures that JB is very skilled at tracking," added Beverly. "We have two weeks. What have we got to lose?"

"We can start narrowing things down right now," said Kate as she opened Google Earth on her laptop, and the group gathered to look.

Charlie, who was most familiar with the area, pointed out the areas of development along the Kenai River and suggested areas that might have sniper potential. "It looks like there are undeveloped stretches of the river at both the east and west ends of Skilac Lake. According to Michael's information from Taylor's Chief of Staff, one of the guided trips will be on the river reach between the lake and a subdivision about eight miles downstream. I'm guessing that this is our most promising area to explore."

"It looks like it would be possible to park in the eastern-most subdivision and hike overland to a secluded area on the north bank of the river," added Beverly. "A hike of one to two miles would probably be reasonable."

"There are several areas of elevated cut bank that would provide good views of the river and concealment at the top," JB said as he removed his sweatshirt, revealing another of his many Grateful Dead T-shirts. "We could start exploring the area in the next couple of days."

"Kate and I have some PI stuff to do," Beverly said as she refilled coffee cups, "so JB and Charlie may be up to bat."

"Well, OK. If you guys want to miss out on trekking through Alaska's beautiful wilderness, that's your loss," said JB. "Are you free tomorrow, Charlie?"

"Yeah. Tomorrow might be good for starters. I suspect this effort may take several days if there is going to be any chance of success."

"It looks like we have a plan of sorts," added Beverly.

"Unfortunately, if plan A fails, we will still need a plan B," Vandorn pointed out. "I guess I can look into the possibility of acquiring some kind of realistic dummy to sit in for Taylor."

"Some might argue that Taylor is already a dummy," quipped JB.

AFTER THE IMPROMPTU MEETING of the four Mooseketeers plus one, Charlie and Michael drove to the trooper's office. They found Bob Stillwater hunched over his crappy desk, looking dejectedly at a pile of papers.

"The fucking paperwork gets worse every year," said the Super Trooper as he looked up at his visitors. "The FBI guys flew the coop and left me to follow up on the investigation, not to mention take the heat when the murderer is not found. What can I do for you guys? I hope you've figured out who done it."

"Anything new from the forensic folks?" asked Michael.

"No," answered Bob. "Ballistics on the bullet in the boat door frame came back with no known matches, and the unknown fingerprint belonged to one of the harbor staff in Washington. We sorta have nothing to go on."

"So, the FBI just left with no word?"

"Yep," answered Bob. "It was very odd. They stormed into Homer like gang busters, pushing everybody around, then suddenly left. I guess I'm back in charge, unfortunately."

"It sounds like the powers-that-be are trying to sweep everything under the rug," said Charlie. "Have there been any reporters around?"

"No. Even the reporters have gone," Bob said.

"That suggests that they have been told to back off by someone with a whole lot of clout, since reporters are usually pretty determined," suggested Michael.

"Yeah, it just gets weirder and weirder," said Charlie as he got up to leave. "By the way, you need to get a new calendar."

CHAPTER 23

AT SIX O'CLOCK THE next morning, Charlie and JB got into Charlie's beat-up SUV and headed north on the Sterling Highway. The road paralleled the east shore of Cook Inlet with occasional expansive views of the snow-capped mountains of the Alaska Range on the other side. The onshore wind and salt air had the effect of limiting tree growth along the coastal strip, leaving only grass, alders, and various low-growing herbaceous species. The unencumbered view was at times spectacular. They drove for about an hour, passing the roadside towns of Ninilchik, Clam Gulch, and Nikiski. The Russian names reflected both the early Russian history of Alaska and the later settlement of the area by Russian Old Believers, a splinter group of the Russian Orthodox Church.

The highway crossed the Kenai River and made a sharp turn to the east at the town of Soldotna, continuing in an easterly direction, roughly parallel to the river on its north side. After an additional five miles, they found the side road to the south marked on Charlie's map and entered a subdivision of recreational cabins on or near the river. They parked out of sight on an untraveled side road that seemed like it would be the most logical place for the sniper to begin his trek southeastward toward the river. It was also a logical place for JB and Charlie to cross the assassin's path, assuming that such a path actually existed.

"Unfortunately, I don't see any fresh car tracks on the road, so this might not have been the starting point for Krupp's explorations," JB said as he donned his daypack. "But if we head southeast, it would seem reasonable that we could cross the assassin's path before he reached the river."

"Yeah," added Charlie as he headed into the dense woods, tripping over windfall spruce branches. "The vegetation here really sucks."

The two snoopy Homeroids plunged into an area that had likely been cleared years previously, but was overgrown with devil's club, alders, and young trees. Within a few hundred feet, they broke out of the undergrowth onto an area of muskeg—wet, boggy terrain—which was almost as bad. Each step sank into the sphagnum and tried to suck their boots off. The uneven, hummocky ground was tricky to navigate and required exceptional balance to remain upright.

"This area brings back unpleasant memories from my past," remarked JB as he nearly fell over. "On one training exercise, my group had to cross a mangrove swamp. The roots and branches were a tangled barrier, and the ground was nothing but muck. That was the most difficult forward progress I've ever encountered on overland travel. This is almost as bad."

"It looks like things are going to get better in a minute," said Charlie as he looked at the satellite image on his GPS. Soon, the muskeg gave way to rising ground. "If we head south, we should hit the river in about fifteen minutes."

Larger spruce and a few birch dominated the natural old-growth forest on the higher ground. The sparse undergrowth made walking much more pleasant, while JB searched for signs that someone had passed by recently.

"I think we may have just become very lucky!" JB excitedly remarked. "Look at these broken branches and faint footprints."

JB was able to follow a faint trail heading southeast, toward the river, as expected. The GPS indicated they were only a few hundred feet from the river, but once again, the vegetation became very dense.

At last, they were able to see daylight through the trees, suggesting a break in the landscape.

"Look at this!" exclaimed Charlie as he pointed to the red flagging tied to a twig. "That either means we're getting close to our sniper nest, or some surveyor was way off the beaten path."

They entered a zone of dense spruce saplings and crawled under the canopy until they almost fell off the edge of the cut bank above the turquoise river. Two more pieces of flagging directed them to Stanley Krupp's carefully selected assassin's vantage point.

"This is it. Looks like we've found our needle in the spruce forest. The branches have been trimmed to make room for a prone body. The view of the river is perfect for sniping, but it's well screened from above and would be almost invisible from a boat," added JB.

"Wow! I sorta can't believe it. Let's try and figure out what our move might be to thwart the shooter."

"Obviously, we'll need to get here before he does and catch him before the VP floats by. But the vegetation is so dense that it might not be easy."

"And who is going to do the actual capturing? The Secret Service is not going to want us lowly civilians to be involved, and we don't have law enforcement credentials," asked Charlie.

"We should discuss that with Michael Vandorn. He might be able to convince the powers-that-be to let us do the capture because of my security clearance and past status. Plus, the Secret Service may be compromised. Beverly's credentials as a former law enforcement officer may also help."

———◆———

THE NEXT FEW DAYS were eerily quiet. For the most part, the Homer crew went about their normal daily business. Michael Vandorn conferred with selected colleagues from the Seattle Federal Prosecutor's office who, in turn, had secret discussions with the head of Vice President Taylor's Secret Service staff. Despite concerns from the Secret

Service and hesitancy from the VP, it was agreed that the Homer citizens involved with uncovering the conspiracy should take the lead in attempting to thwart the plot to assassinate VP Taylor. The extreme nature of the conspiracy seemed to dictate that extraordinary, even extralegal, measures were justified. The Vice President was not happy and came close to calling off the whole fishing trip, but eventually politics ruled the day. He was persuaded that he would come out of the situation as a hero, assuming that he did not end up dead.

Chapter 24

Two Weeks Later

IN THE EARLY AFTERNOON on August fifth, the day before the vice president's fishing trip, Charlie, JB, and Beverly traveled from Homer up the highway past Soldotna to the rustic subdivision that provided an approach to the assassin nest. They parked along a street in an area with cabins so that the shooter would not be spooked by the presence of a vehicle near his secluded spot on the unused side road. The need to park in an out-of-the-way spot meant an extra half mile of hiking.

They saw no sign of a car as they approached the likely forest entry point and concluded that the gunman had probably not yet arrived. Information provided by the vice president's chief of staff suggested that the VP's boat would likely pass the sniper nest at about ten o'clock the next morning. There was no way of knowing whether the shooter would come early and spend the night in his nest, or whether he would come early the next morning. Regardless, the Mooseketeers needed to be on site first, so they were taking no chances. It seemed like they had no choice but to spend the night in the woods, ensuring that they would be in position before the shooter arrived, either that evening or in the morning.

Each carried a pack with essentials for spending the night, and each was armed—JB and Beverly carried their favorite handguns, and Charlie carried a twelve-gauge shotgun. The trio roughly followed the path taken earlier by JB and Charlie. When they reached the river-bank, they plotted a strategy for capturing the shooter. Early in the morning, they would position themselves in a triangle adjacent to the sniper nest with JB and Beverly one hundred feet upstream and downstream, respectively, along the riverbank, while Charlie would move in behind the shooter. If all proceeded according to plan, the Mooseketeers would close in from three sides. The steep bank would likely block escape toward the river.

After reviewing their roles, the three retreated from the sniper nest and set up a temporary camp to await the morning. Radio contact with Vice President Taylor's head of the Secret Service was tested and found to be working properly.

———•———

Dick Whelan emerged from his hotel room in Homer at three o'clock on assassination day and drove north. Dawn was just begin-ning to break as he reached his destination at the edge of the woods. He carried a large pack that contained his rifle, an insulating blanket to fool any attempt at infrared sensing from above, and other items to assure comfort while waiting for his quarry to pass by.

Using his GPS, he retraced his path to the sniper nest. As before, hiking was difficult through the dense vegetation. Two expletive-laden hours later, he crawled under the tree canopy to his cozy shooting site. He positioned the rifle the way he wanted it, pulled the blanket over himself and settled in for a long wait.

His anonymous contact had informed him that the target was the Vice President of the United States, and that he would likely be in the first of two boats that would float by his location at about ten o'clock. Whelan had given much thought to how he would escape after shooting such an important person. He ultimately decided that trying to leave the area immediately after the shot would not work. The police and Secret Service would seal off all avenues of escape. He decided it would be better to hide and wait it out until things had cooled down. Whelan's earlier explorations found a hiding spot in a small cave under a rock outcrop about one-half mile from the sniper nest. He figured that would protect him from aerial surveillance and shelter him from the weather. He stashed enough supplies in his secret cave to last several days. He figured he would be in good shape unless dogs were used to track him. In that case, he would be totally screwed.

———◆———

THE DAY OF THE vice president's fishing trip dawned clear and bright, with air temperature forecast to be in the mid-seventies—warm for the Kenai Peninsula in the summer. It looked like it was going to be a beautiful day.

VP Taylor had arrived in Anchorage two days prior, hosting several fundraising events at the Captain Cook Hotel before traveling in a motorcade of three SUVs to an upscale fishing lodge on a promontory overlooking the Kenai River. Taylor hosted another fundraiser for prominent sportsmen and politicos, accompanied by drinking that continued until late into the night. After closing down the lodge bar, Taylor, his chief of staff, and head of the Secret Service detail met secretly in Taylor's room to review plans for the next day.

At seven o'clock the following morning, Vice President Taylor, along with two Secret Service agents, a fishing guide, and Mark Anderson, local constituent and fishing buddy, walked down to the lodge dock and got into two outboard-powered drift boats. To say that Taylor was not enthusiastic about the fishing excursion was an understatement. Acting as sniper bait was not high on his list of favorite things. He had been skeptical of reliance on the odd citizen posse to catch the bad guy before he was able to fulfill his mission. But his chief of security had convinced him that it would be the safest option.

As the VP and his entourage embarked onto the blue-green river, they looked like an advertisement for Cabela's, all decked out in crisp, new camouflage outdoor clothing. It was doubtful whether the fish were impressed by the camo gear. The first boat was operated by the guide and contained the VP and his chief of security, while the second contained Anderson and the other agents. The boats motored out into the milky blue-green water and began the trip upstream to selected fishy locations. The plan was to motor nearly up to Skilak Lake, then drift back downstream. Fishing opportunities abounded, including salmon and trophy rainbow trout.

————◆————

Dick Whelan, having arrived just after dawn at the sniper nest, was snacking on a granola bar as he lay facing the river. He was comfortable and warm in his nest with a camouflaged blanket over his body and his rifle. It was about nine o'clock, and he expected the Vice President to be floating past his position in about an hour if the schedule given to him by Krupp was correct. He checked his range-finder and made some final adjustments to the rifle scope.

He was feeling confident and relaxed when he heard a rustling noise off to his left. Thinking it was probably a moose, he peeked out from under the blanket and saw a flash of a brown jacket. At the same time, a voice yelled for him not to move. What the fuck? He turned and fired the rifle toward the noise without aiming. Immediately, two shots from a small-caliber handgun ripped through the leaves. A third shot from a more powerful handgun was fired from the other side, followed by a very loud boom behind him from what sounded like a shotgun.

He was scared and obviously in trouble, trapped between the steep riverbank and at least three pursuers. Thinking he had no choice, he pushed out from the trees, leaving his gear behind and jumped off the edge of the bluff. The angle of repose of the eroded bluff above the river was so steep that he flew about ten feet through the air before hitting the silty bank, skidded downward on his heels, lost his balance, and did a face plant at the river's edge. His momentum caused him to roll into the deep, rapidly moving water. He panicked as his heavy clothing weighed him down and the current started to carry him downstream.

Suddenly, a gangly apparition with wild hair grabbed his jacket and pulled him out of the water. Before he could think, his Glock was removed from his holster and his hands were cuffed behind his back.

———◆———

I can hear him, texted JB to Charlie and Beverly. JB lay near the edge of the riverbank about one hundred feet from the sniper nest. The Mooseketeers had moved into position just before dawn and were waiting for the shooter to appear. The basic plan was to move in as fast as possible and, hopefully, surprise the shooter. The gunman would obviously be armed with a rifle, but a scoped long gun would not be ideal at short range in the forest. But the odds were good that he would also have a handgun, and they wanted to get things under control swiftly.

OK. Let's approach, texted Charlie.

Charlie, Beverly, and JB quietly moved toward the presumed sniper in a three-pronged pincer movement.

"Don't move!" yelled JB when he was about thirty feet away and in sight of the shooter. "We have you covered from three directions."

Whelan pivoted and fired one unaimed rifle shot toward JB. The bullet ripped through the branches a few feet from JB, who responded with two shots from his Beretta, both of which were intercepted by vegetation. At the same time, Beverly fired toward the sniper nest even though she was unable to see the shooter, and Charlie fired his shotgun into the air.

The gunman totally surprised JB by ditching his rifle and jumping off the edge of the bluff onto the steep mud bank above the river. Whelan landed feet first, skidding down the slope, but was not able to keep his balance and toppled headfirst, landing near the river and rolling into the water. Charlie and Beverly crashed through the trees just as Whelan entered the water. Beverly shot twice but missed the rapidly moving target.

Meanwhile, JB followed the shooter over the edge, jumping nearly halfway down the slope. He managed to stay on his feet as he skidded on his heels down the slippery mud slope, coming to a halt at the water's edge. Knowing that the fast-flowing river would carry the shooter downstream, JB adjusted his jump to lead the shooter and ended up grabbing a sputtering Whelan and pulling him out of the water. Whelan's handgun was still in his holster—he had not had time to unholster the gun. JB quickly removed the Glock from the shivering gunman as he lay on the ground and cuffed his hands behind his back with flex cuffs. The cold water and heavy, waterlogged clothing rendered the shooter nearly helpless. Whelan shivered at the edge of the river, looking totally defeated.

Charlie and Beverly slowly and carefully descended the bank and met up with JB and his soggy prisoner. Charlie notified Taylor's Chief of Security by radio and asked where the boats were located on the river. It turned out that the fishermen were upstream and would be at their location in about fifteen minutes to pick up the sniper.

Beverly climbed back up the steep bank and retrieved Whelan's rifle, pack, and blanket. The blanket was wrapped around the humiliated hypothermic sniper, and they settled down to wait for the vice president's entourage.

CHAPTER 25

The two boats carrying the vice president's fishing entourage came around the bend, saw the group of Homeroids on the bank with their prisoner, and pulled in at a gravel bar immediately downstream. Charlie and JB led the prisoner to the boat, where custody of the assassin was taken over by the secret service agents. Whelan was secured to the seat. Charlie joined the VP in his boat while JB and Beverly joined the agents and Whelan. Both boats pushed back out into the current and began to motor downstream.

"I'm fucking cold," exclaimed Whelan, still wrapped in the blanket.

"Gee. Too bad," retorted one agent. "We'll get you some dry clothes when we get to the lodge."

In the VP's boat, Taylor sat in the middle seat facing Charlie. He was shaking with the aftermath of an adrenaline peak.

"You guys are pretty amazing," said the VP as he drank from a silver flask pulled from a jacket pocket. "How did you know where the sniper was going to be?"

"We were very lucky. JB's an experienced tracker, and we happened to cross his trail."

"Well, I owe you guys my life. How is it that a few citizens from Alaska were able to accomplish things that my secret service detail couldn't?"

"I guess we were just in the right place at the right time."

About twenty minutes later, they pulled into the lodge dock, which had been cleared of all activity except for two waiting Secret Service agents. One of the agents had reluctantly agreed to donate clothing so the assassin would not become hypothermic on route to the Kenai jail. As an additional insult, Whelan had to strip naked behind a tree and replace his clothes while being watched by the big, burly agents. One of the VP's ridiculously large SUVs was used to transport the shooter. Local law enforcement authorities were notified that Whelan's transgressions were none of their business, and the Secret Service would handle things. Needless to say, the local cops were not happy, but they were clearly outgunned politically.

Whelan, probably not his real name, was not saying anything, which was alright with the vice president and his loyal protection detail. The conspiracy had cast doubt on who they could trust, and Whelan's silence made it easier to limit knowledge of his capture and increased the likelihood of truncating the conspiracy.

CHARLIE, BEVERLY, AND JB were dismissed by the Secret Service as soon as they reached the Kenai jail. They were not sure whether they were being kept out of the jail process because of secrecy or embarrassment that citizens were doing their job. But anonymity was fine with them. On the way into Homer, they stopped at Trooper headquarters, even though they had been warned not to talk to local authorities. Bob was glumly sitting at his desk, working on endless paperwork as usual.

"What's up?" asked Bob.

"We've had a pretty interesting day, which we unfortunately can't talk about," said Charlie. "But we thought we would give you a heads up about a part of it. As it happens, there is an individual in custody in Kenai you may want to question about Vandorn's murder. You may be especially interested in the ballistics of his nine mm Glock. He's currently under the control of the U.S. Secret Service, so cooperation may be difficult. But you have a pretty compelling reason for wanting to examine the gun. It's certainly worth a try."

"That sounds intriguing and weird," replied Bob. "I'm guessing this all has something to do with the vice president's fishing trip, since that's the only reason I can see that the Secret Service would be involved."

"We can neither confirm nor deny your guess," said Beverly with a wink.

"Maybe a way to get around the secrecy would be for you to suggest that an anonymous citizen reported a prisoner being transported by the feds, and you were wondering what was going on," said Charlie.

"What makes you think this guy may be involved?" asked Bob.

"He's probably a gun for hire, and there may be overlap with some of the people involved in today's activities," answered Charlie.

"How do you guys get involved in this stuff?" asked Bob.

"I guess we're just lucky or stupid," replied Beverly. "And when are you going to get rid of that sexist calendar?"

"What can I say? I like it." Bob said as he swept all the papers on his desk into one pile and pushed them aside. "The heck with this. I'm going to try to do some actual law enforcement work. I know the deputy at the jail. I'll give him a call and see if I can get contact information for the feds. Thanks for the heads up."

"Good luck with that," said Charlie as he got up to leave. "We'll fill you in as soon as we can. See you later."

Back at the Shearwater, Kate and Michael Vandorn were waiting for word on the events of the day. Beer and chips were passed around to the famished crew.

"So, what do we do now?" asked Kate after hearing about the crazy day.

"I have a strong feeling that someone from the VP's security detail is going to be calling soon for a debriefing," said Charlie. "I guess we'll take it from there."

"Michael, do you have any idea what your role in this will be?" asked Beverly.

"I really don't have a clue."

———◆———

"WHAT THE FUCK HAPPENED?" yelled Senator Strunk over his secure satellite phone. "The VP is supposed to be dead."

"I'm not really sure, Elmore," replied Stanley Krupp. "Events are very hazy. My informants in Kenai said they saw a couple of black SUVs pull into the Kenai jail and unload at least one person. A couple of Secret Service types watched while someone remained in the vehicle, presumably the vice president. Additionally, three apparent civilians left in another car and headed back to the highway. I'm totally at a loss. I can only assume that our assassin has been jailed."

"Well, that's just fuckin' great. How could anyone have known what we were doing? And, how much more do they know? We could all be totally screwed."

"I'm trying to find out as much as I can."

After the senator hung up, Stanley paced in front of his picture window overlooking the little lake outside his cabin. How indeed, thought Stanley. Although members of the group knew the basics of the plan, only two people knew the location and exact timing of the proposed assassination—himself and the shooter. It was unlikely the shooter would implicate himself. He could maybe understand how his sniper could get captured after the fact, but not before. If the VP had been injured, it would be all over the news. It seemed unlikely that the sniper could have missed completely at such short range. So, somehow, he had probably been captured before or during the act. Stanley had a bad feeling that the complications were somehow linked to the missing document, which gave hints of the assassination plan. But, even so, more detailed information and local knowledge would have been required to find the sniper nest.

Was someone listening in on his conversations? A listening device in his cabin seemed highly unlikely—or maybe not. What other explanation could there be? Stanley began to search. After about twenty minutes, he was about to give up when he looked at the switch plate on the wall near the door. Removing the plate, he was surprised to actually find what appeared to be a sophisticated recorder. *Holy shit! I actually found something.* He was about to remove it when he thought about fingerprints. He put on gloves and retrieved the device, carefully putting it into a Ziploc bag. His FBI friends could look for prints and maybe get other information from the device. A wireless connection likely had to be employed to retrieve the information. Maybe a phone number could be retrieved.

His observer at the Kenai jail thought he recognized one of the civilians who emerged from the motorcade as a Homer resident. Stanley was hoping that information from the listening device could be used to identify the snoop, making elimination of the problem much easier.

The rest of the Project Nemesis team needed to be informed of the disastrous events, but Stanley was not looking forward to their response. How much information had leaked? Members' names? A mole within the team seemed like another possibility. If there was a spy, then everyone was in danger. Stanley figured they would likely find out pretty quickly if that were the case. He began to think in terms of escape. He had a ditch kit in his plane and contingency plans for getting out of Dodge if necessary. He would let things play out a little longer.

Meanwhile, he needed to courier the listening device to Washington immediately. Stanley got in his plane and flew to a private airstrip close to Soldotna and drove to the nearest UPS store.

Chapter 26

THE MORNING AFTER THE wild day on the Kenai River was rainy and dismal. Charlie was exhausted from sleeping on the ground the night before, not to mention chasing an assassin into the river. The sound of rain hitting the deck above Charlie's cabin in the Shearwater was soothing, and he slept late. Kate had left hours earlier for her job at FlashFrozen.

He was just sitting down to a cup of coffee in the galley when his phone rang. He glanced at the "unlisted number" indication on his phone screen. He thought, *shit! I'm not even awake yet.* The Secret Service was on the way and wanted to talk. He alerted JB, Beverly and Michael Vandorn, suggesting they join the party.

Thirty minutes later, all participants were crowded into the small cabin of the Shearwater. Ralph Neff, head of the vice president's security detail, was the guest of honor. He was a tall, fit man who looked exactly like the clean-cut Secret Service stereotypes depicted in the movies. Beverly could not help but wonder how they managed to find so many people who looked alike. Introductions were made, and coffee was passed around.

"Ok, so where are we at?" asked Charlie, looking at Neff.

"Well, I wish I knew," responded Neff. "Our assassin is still incarcerated in Kenai. We don't quite know what to do with him, given the fact that we don't know who to trust at this stage. He will probably be moved to federal custody in Seattle later today, but once that happens, a lot more people will be in the loop. I want you to know that the vice president is very appreciative. Needless to say, the Secret Service is somewhat embarrassed by the whole thing, but I'm personally glad you were around. It would help me a lot if you guys could start at the beginning and fill me in on everything you know."

Beverly, as a former federal law enforcement officer, took the lead and ran through the sequence of events, starting with Aldo's nocturnal visit and ending with Michael Vandorn's recent surveillance of the visitor to his boat.

"Wow. You guys have been busy," said Neff as he sipped his coffee. "I imagine you've broken numerous laws, but I don't give a shit since it probably saved the VP's life. The involvement of Senator Strunk is an especially scary prospect since he wields a lot of influence with the intelligence community. I don't relish the thought of getting crosswise with him."

"I guess the big question is what happens from here?" said Michael. "Selected people in the prosecutor's office and the VP's staff have heard our recording of the conspirators and have images of their faces. Are these people going to be rounded up and arrested, or will politics get in the way?"

"The answer to your question is above my pay grade," answered Neff. "I don't even know if the president has been notified, but I'm assuming he has. The Secret Service is sometimes pretty isolated from the other agencies and has its own internal issues."

"I'm concerned that some of us may be in danger," said Charlie. "I suspect that Stanley Krupp is a smart and resourceful man with a lot to lose if his plans go sideways. If he has spies in Kenai, he will know that JB, Beverly, and I were involved in foiling the assassination. Also, we don't have a good handle on who killed Michael's brother and why. Krupp apparently was not aware of Richard Vandorn's murder. But it seems likely that Senator Strunk may have played a part. The senator may have his own agenda, apart from the conspirators."

"I have a bit of new information," added Beverly. "Kate and I have been researching Krupp's consulting company, ironically called Gentle Persuasion. Their website was pretty sketchy, but military contractors seem to be the primary clients."

"Why am I not surprised?" quipped JB. "The plot thickens."

"So, JB, have you heard anything more from your old boss?" asked Charlie.

"Who was your old boss?" asked Neff.

"I can't tell you."

"JB has a mysterious past," replied Beverly.

"The answer is no, I haven't heard from him, but I'm expecting something soon. He may be our best bet for inside information at the Washington D.C. level."

"Shit, you guys have more resources than the FBI," said Ralph Neff. "I did a background search on all of you, and JB apparently didn't exist until he was 28 years old. I don't even want to know what he was doing. But you guys do need to be careful."

"During the meeting that JB and Beverly overheard, it was mentioned that the Homeland Security secretary, Gloria Alvarez, may be the next in line for elimination," Charlie said. "It seems like it would be a good idea to protect her."

"That's already being done," answered Neff. "The problem is we couldn't use the Secret Service since it's almost certain that someone in the service is in cahoots with the conspirators. So, we hired a private security contractor, who will hopefully limit knowledge of the special security to my staff. But a leak is probably inevitable for such a prominent person."

"So, what you're saying is knowledge of the conspiracy will soon be all over Washington," suggested Charlie.

"Yeah. I don't see how we avoid that."

"Michael, as a lawyer, would it be possible to round up and arrest all of these guys based on our recording of their involvement?" asked Charlie as Buster the cat, oblivious to the seriousness of the conversation, jumped onto the galley table.

"If these guys were domestic or foreign terrorists, they would be in big trouble. But, since they're politicians or government employees, it would probably take more than remarks at a summer cabin get-together to convict. They could say they were just engaged in wishful thinking during a drunken afternoon. A direct tie of one of the members to the assassin would likely change things. Another aspect is the fact that Senator Strunk was not at the meeting. He may well be the most important member. Plus, a major loose end is the murder of my brother. We don't even know if it was connected to the conspiracy."

"I have a bit of bad news," offered JB as Buster settled on his lap. "I queried the listening device in Krupp's cabin last night, and it seems to be no longer operating. So, it's either broken or Krupp found it. I'm guessing the latter. I wiped my fingerprints before hiding it, but I suppose it could somehow be traced to me through my phone number, the website I bought it from, or maybe even DNA, given the resources available to these guys. We could be in the crosshairs of Krupp and company."

"Great," moaned Beverly.

"We've been here before," said JB. "We can enlist the community to help along with our friend Gertie at Homer's sleaziest bar."

"I've rigged up Richard's boat to detect intruders, which may help," added Michael.

"OK, we need to keep in touch," Ralph Neff suggested as he stood up to leave. "Thanks for keeping the vice president alive, not to mention preventing a lot of embarrassment to the Secret Service and allowing me to keep my job. You guys are a major force of nature. Things could be happening quickly from now on, so be careful."

<h1 style="text-align:center">CHAPTER 27</h1>

Three days later

"GOOD MORNING, ELMORE. WHAT'VE you got for me?" Stanley Krupp said as he settled into his easy chair and put his phone on speaker. It was a beautiful late summer morning in the Caribou Hills. Unfortunately, Stanley's mood was not so bright.

"The good news is I think we found the identity of one of the guys who helped fuck up our plans," replied Senator Strunk. "There were no fingerprints on the listening device you sent, but my tech guy was able to retrieve the phone number used to access the device. It belongs to a guy named Johann Sebastian Bachman, currently living in Homer. Mr. Bachman is an interesting guy. It looks like he worked for the government when he was in his twenties, but his records are sealed tighter than a drum—maybe black ops. He has a Ph.D. in political science and worked as a professor at USC in California until about five years ago. He was fired because of an affair with a student and moved to Homer. In short, this guy probably has intelligence and maybe military training."

"That's just great. How the heck did he get involved?"

"I have no idea. You're closer to the action than I am."

"Yeah, yeah. Has there been anything going on in Washington? Are any of our guys being hassled?"

"No. The vice president's office has been completely quiet. As far as I know, the media hasn't gotten word of the assassination attempt yet. They're keeping things under wraps for now."

"I guess that's good, but we need to do something as soon as possible to put a lid on things. Obviously, there are several people in Washington and Alaska who know what's going on. I've got a man in Homer who can do some research on Bachman. Maybe find out who his associates are. We can think about what to do after that."

"OK. But let's not think too long. Our future lives may be at stake," said Senator Strunk as he ended the call.

Stanley thought for a minute, then called John Melman, his Homer contact.

"Why is there so much noise?" asked Stanley.

"I'm sitting in a bar," yelled Melman into the phone.

"Well, go outside so we can talk privately," replied Stanley as he thought to himself that trusting Melman might not be such a good idea. He was not the brightest bulb in the chandelier. Hopefully, he would be able to accomplish simple tasks, such as basic surveillance.

"Ok, I'm outside."

"We need you to find out all you can about a guy from Homer named Johann Bachman and then follow him to get an idea of his habits and friends."

"How do I do that?"

"You're at a bar. First, I'd ask some of your drinking buddies if they have heard of him. Homer's a pretty small town, so you may be able to find out where he lives. If not, keep looking. Once you find him, start surveillance to find out his habits and friends, and anything else interesting. And keep quiet."

"OK. I can do that."

"Give me a call as soon as you locate him."

———◆———

JOHN MELMAN TOOK A few minutes to digest Krupp's instructions, then went back into Gertie's Bar, ordered another beer, and sat at a table with several fellow slackers. He immediately struck gold. One of his buddies had heard of a guy named Bachman who hung out at the harbor on a sailboat with a funny name, something with Otter in the name. His friend thought that most people called Bachman JB.

Melman could not believe his luck. Maybe this spy stuff was easier than he thought. He fired up his old Chevy Blazer and drove to the harbor. Observing from above, it was pretty easy to pick out the piers where most of the sailboats were docked. Since boat names were mostly written on the transoms, Melman walked up and down the docks, looking across to the adjacent piers and reading the names of all the sailboats. On his fourth transit, he saw a boat with the name, *Otterly Ridiculous*. *That's got to be it*, Melman thought. *What a stupid name.*

He walked around the boat and cleverly deduced from all the stuff piled on the deck that the boat was probably a live-aboard. But there was no sign of an occupant, and it had an abandoned feeling. A large man two boats down from the *Otterly Ridiculous* was working on the deck of his powerboat.

"Hey, man. Do you know anything about the owner of that sailboat?" asked Melman.

"No, I think he moved out of state."

"Oh. OK, thanks," replied Melman. As he left the harbor, it occurred to him that he might have just blown the whole secrecy thing. If the guy was telling the truth, then there was nothing more he could do, and if the guy was lying, he just effectively alerted Bachman that someone was looking for him.

Melman tried to think of ways to get more information on the sailboat's owner, but he came up empty. He could ask the harbormaster, but that would be too obvious. He could spy on the boat, but if the guy was gone, that would be useless. He thought maybe state boat registrations could help, but did not know where to start. Besides, his computer was broken. Out of options, he returned to Gertie's Bar to think about it.

———•———

"IT LOOKS LIKE KRUPP and company have identified JB," said Charlie as he sat down next to Kate at the settee in the galley of the *Shearwater*. Kate had just arrived from another long day at FlashFrozen. Both had beers, and a large bag of potato chips occupied the space between them. Buster purred on Kate's lap. "Our friend John Melman was snooping around the *Otterly Ridiculous* and stupidly asked me where the owner was. I said that JB was out of town. I recognized Melman from your driver's license photo. He isn't exactly sneaky."

"Great, so what do we do now?" mumbled Kate with a mouth full of chips.

"I called JB a few minutes ago, and we're all going to meet at his place after dinner. It's probably just a matter of time before Melman figures out where JB lives, and we need to be prepared."

Two hours later, the four Moosketeers plus Michael Vandorn were comfortably seated in Beverly's living room.

"I guess this is a council of war," said JB as he sipped a whisky.

"I think it's more a council of how to keep JB and the rest of us alive," replied Kate.

"JB, what have you learned from the recorder in Melman's cabin and the tracker on his car?" asked Michael.

"Nothing on the cabin recorder, so he must have gotten calls while at Gertie's, where he spends most of his time. Unsurprisingly, the tracker on the Blazer shows him going to the harbor and back and forth to Gertie's."

"I called Gertie, and she said that he's been circulating around the bar talking to various people, presumably to get more information," Charlie said as he mixed himself a strong drink.

"Michael, what have you heard from the nation's capital?" asked Beverly.

"Not a word. I was hoping to get feedback from my boss at the prosecutor's office in Seattle, but he hasn't heard anything either. Things are way too quiet. I wish we had a better way of getting information."

"I'll contact my old boss, Karl, again and see if he has heard any rumors through the D.C. intelligence grapevine," JB said.

Chapter 28

Secretary of Homeland Security, Gloria Alvarez, lounged on the overstuffed white leather couch in her Arlington, Virginia home. Birch logs blazed in her stone fireplace. Her German shepherd, Attila, lay next to her with his head on her lap. Gloria was an attractive woman, tall and slender with dark eyes, long raven black hair, and a perfect complexion. She was also tough and whip smart. Her grandparents had crossed the border illegally into the U.S. in the 1940s to escape the cartel presence in central Mexico. Her abuela was pregnant with her mother when they crossed the border. Her grandfather, and then her father, managed a successful construction business in East Texas. Gloria was the first of three children and by far the smartest of the Alvarez siblings. To everybody's amazement, Gloria graduated from a Texas state college and was accepted at Harvard Law School. Her first job was in the legal department of the FBI, where she worked herself up to the level of a senior legal analyst. Along the way, she had passed through the full agent training program at Quantico. The president had appointed her to the Homeland Security Secretary position partly to fulfill diversity requirements in his cabinet, but mostly because he felt that she would fall into line with his policies. He had seriously underestimated her independence.

Since being informed of a possible assassination plot against her, she was understandably a nervous wreck. As she sipped her Glenlivet double malt on the rocks, she was trying to make sense of the whole thing. Gloria was painfully aware that she had enemies in the government and was not altogether surprised by the revelations. The Homeland Security Department was a morass of political intrigue and petty jealousies. But the way in which she had been informed was puzzling, and the strong suggestion of secrecy, even relating to her own staff, was disconcerting.

She had been informed directly by the Vice President, bypassing her Secret Service detail, and warned about leaking word of the threat to anyone but the most trusted personnel. All of which clearly indicated that the threat was from within. But the scariest part was that she did not trust her own security detail either. Little things over the last few months had suggested that some members of her Secret Service detail were discussing things that should not be discussed. It was just a feeling—women's intuition. So, here she was. Advised to take precautions, but not knowing who to trust. Private security had been added to her protection detail, but it would be impossible to prevent the Secret Service from speculating about the reasons since their job was to notice the little things.

One name that kept popping into her head was Elmore Strunk. She and the senator had clashed numerous times. Besides differing political philosophies, Senator Strunk was a loathsome individual, combining racism, misogyny, and crude behavior all in one package. If the threat originated from Washington, D.C., she was sure the senator was somehow involved.

So, what the fuck to do? She ultimately concluded that she would have to take care of herself. In a past life, she had gone through the rigorous FBI academy. She was pretty sure she could handle herself in most situations. She had a good home security system and could probably depend to some extent on her security detail. But she did not have the benefit of advance security in her movements, like the president. She was well aware that modern snipers could hit targets at distances of more than a half mile. There was no way to protect against every contingency.

Gloria's approach to life was data-driven, and she badly needed more information. She gathered from her conversation with the VP that some civilians in Alaska had initially uncovered the plot. But that was all she knew. She was determined to find out more about these folks, and she had some ideas how she might do that. After all, she had the total resources of the U.S. Government at her disposal.

Gloria sat back, took another sip of scotch, and picked up her latest spy novel. She reflexively reached under the throw pillow next to her to make sure her loaded Glock was still there.

———— ◆ ————

SENATOR STRUNK WAS ENGAGED in diametrically opposite ruminations. Coincidentally, like Gloria, he was sipping expensive scotch on the rocks in front of a roaring fire in his Arlington home, but his thoughts turned to ways in which Gloria Alvarez's life could be terminated without blowing back on him. The participants in Project Nemesis had already fucked up beyond belief, mandating that his first concern was self-preservation. He had not attended the Alaska meeting intentionally, thereby giving him some deniability. He hoped to take advantage of the fact that the conspiracy had apparently already been unveiled. If he played his cards right, he might be able to blame any further nefarious acts on the bunch of bozos that he had initially recruited to his cause.

He needed to find another person to carry out his lethal plans, specifically someone willing to operate in the more urban confines of the Washington, D.C. area. He decided to bypass Stanley Krupp this time since the assassination of the vice president had been so fucked up. One of his former associates in the intelligence community was familiar with the dark web options and was tasked with the job of finding a willing hitman. He wrote an encrypted message to his colleague, providing the target and specifications for such a hit.

———◆———

The following day, Gloria sat in her office along with her most trusted young analyst, Phillip, who happened to be fluent in all the many databases available to Homeland Security. Her office door was closed and locked, and she had given strict orders not to be disturbed. Gloria had heard through the intelligence grapevine that Senator Strunk's Chief of Staff had been murdered in Homer, Alaska, of all places. His murder had to be connected somehow to the conspiracy to get rid of the vice president and, potentially, herself. Phillip was in the process of getting as much information on Richard Vandorn as he could.

"It seems like Vandorn was a pretty normal, dull congressional staffer," said Phillip. "There's no indication that he was a whacko like the senator. What's abnormal is the lack of information on the investigation of his murder. The FBI was sent to investigate, but that's where the information stops. I guess further investigation was left to the local authorities."

"Does Vandorn have any relatives?"

"The only one I can find is a brother, Michael, who happens to be a federal prosecutor working out of Seattle."

"OK. That's interesting. I assume that the brother would be interested in what's going on with his brother's murder. He could be an entry point into the Alaska situation. Do we have a phone number for him?"

"Yeah, I've got both a mobile number and his office number in the prosecutor's office."

Gloria dialed Michael Vandorn's cell phone using her personal encrypted mobile phone.

"This is Michael."

"Good morning. This is Gloria Alvarez from Washington, D.C."

"Holy cow! Good morning, Madam Secretary," replied Michael.

"No need to be formal. This is a very informal call. Call me Gloria. I'm very sorry for your loss."

"Thank you, Gloria. But I have a feeling that this call isn't about condolences."

"I have a reason to be interested in your brother's murder in Alaska, and I'm looking for more information."

"Before you go any further, I'm aware of the assassination plot against you, so I totally understand your concern."

"I gather you have a lot more information than I do, which is what I was hoping for and is the reason for my call. Have you been in contact with the people from Alaska who uncovered the conspiracy?" asked Gloria.

"Yeah. As it happens, I'm in Homer, Alaska, right now, living on my brother's boat. I've been working closely with the four exceptional people who saved the Vice President's life and secretly gathered intelligence regarding the so-called Project Nemesis. Since you were a primary target, I'm going to make a leap of faith that you're not one of the conspirators. What do you want to know?"

"Basically, I need to know what the fuck is going on so I can protect myself both physically and politically," replied Gloria. "By the way, this call is on a secure phone, so you don't have to worry about anyone listening on my end."

Michael proceeded to relate the events of the last few weeks to Gloria Alvarez. She was, of course, interested in the names of the conspirators, and she was especially interested in Stanley Krupp as a potential ring leader. She had encountered his name before. She agreed to keep Michael in the loop and vice versa. Ending the call, Gloria turned to her assistant.

"Phillip, I want you to covertly find out everything there is to know about Stanley Krupp and his associates using whatever means necessary."

"I'm on it, Boss," he replied.

CHAPTER 29

STANLEY KRUPP WAS GETTING impatient and stressed. On the one hand, he half expected black helicopters to swoop in to his cabin and arrest him any minute. On the other hand, Senator Strunk had assured him that no action was being taken against the known conspirators at this time. Supposedly, the source of information regarding the participants in Project Nemesis was too uncertain for the Feds to take action.

Adding to his stress was the fact that Senator Strunk seemed to be operating on his own to find another assassin to do away with Gloria Alvarez. It was not as if you could order a hit man off the shelf. Closer to home, Melman, his mostly worthless spy in Homer, had made little progress in getting information on Johann (JB) Bachman. On the positive side, Stanley had been able to find an address in Homer for Bachman through connections at the Alaska Permanent Fund Dividend registry. All Alaskans received an annual dividend check from the state's huge savings account. Since few people passed up free money, the registry was a reliable up-to-date record.

Meanwhile, the self-righteous Homer busybodies were running around unchecked, and they obviously knew the location of his cabin, since they had planted the listening device. Stanley really, really wanted to eliminate these annoying Homeroids. But he feared that further violence would just energize any effort to quell his carefully planned coup. Maybe a little fear would help to quiet Bachman and whoever else is involved. He resolved to personally handle any efforts in Homer that might interfere with Project Nemesis.

The following day, Stanley hopped in his plane and flew to Homer. He arranged for John Melman to meet him at the airport. Stanley reasoned that Melman's knowledge of the area and conspicuously inconspicuous trashed Blazer would be useful in prowling around town. Melman provided Krupp with a tour of the area, then drove past the driveway to JB and Beverly's cabin. Because of the long driveway, they could not see the cabin. After parking in an out-of-the-way area off the road, they walked through the meadows of tall grass and alder bushes for several hundred yards until the cabin suddenly came into view, less than a hundred feet away. No cars were in sight.

"Ow, Ow, Ow," yelped Melman as he scratched at his bare arms.

"Nettles," said Stanley.

"I know."

"If you know, then why'd you touch them with bare arms?"

"I forgot."

"It looks like nobody is home," Stanley said. "Maybe we can turn the tables and plant a listening device in Bachman's cabin. I just happen to have one in my pocket."

"Boy, that is sure lucky," replied Melman. Stanley did not know whether Melman was being sarcastic or just stupid. He suspected the latter.

Stanley crept up to the back of the cabin and peered into the kitchen window. No sign of life. The window was open a few inches, and the small listening device was placed behind one of the corners of the screen, mostly out of sight from the inside.

"Your assignment is to find a secluded spot to hide and listen to what is going on whenever there are cars in the drive," said Stanley. "The bug has a range of about one thousand feet, so you'll need to find a location that is both hidden and close enough to be in range. As soon as you hear something useful, give me a call right away."

"That sounds really boring."

"Yeah, surveillance is usually boring, but if you want to get paid, you'll have to deal with it."

"OK. Where are you going to be?"

"I'm headed back to the Caribou Hills, but I can get back to Homer in less than an hour in my plane."

———◆———

"The tracker on Melman's Blazer had some interesting results this morning," JB said to Charlie as he swung aboard the *Shearwater* with his usual flourish. "First, Melman went to the airport, then he drove close to Beverly's cabin and parked for a while. After twenty minutes, he left and went back to the airport and then on to Gertie's Tavern, his home away from home. I'm guessing that he, and whoever he was with, were scouting the place."

"Wow. Were you at home?"

"No. I was stuffing my face at the bakery, and Beverly's out doing PI stuff."

"Obviously, Stanley Krupp comes to mind as someone he might pick up at the airport."

"Exactly what I was thinking. You want to come with me and check things out to see what they were up to? I called Beverly and suggested she stay away until we have a chance to look around."

"Sure. Let's go."

Fifteen minutes later, JB and Charlie pulled into Beverly's neighborhood, drove by the location where Melman had parked earlier, and entered the driveway.

"I guess a bomb is one possibility, so let's proceed carefully," said Charlie.

"I'll go along with that," replied JB. "Also, there could be a listening device, so silence may be in order."

"Roger that."

They proceeded to inspect the outside of the cabin. Two sets of footprints were evident in the dewy vegetation near the house. No trip wires or indication of a bomb were seen. The lock on the trap door to the crawl space had not been tampered with. Charlie motioned to JB and signaled to be quiet. He pointed to the frame of one of the kitchen windows. The listening device was partially visible from the exterior, but would be hard to see from the inside. JB nodded, and they retreated to the car.

"OK. There's a bug. What do we do with it?" whispered Charlie.

"It looks like a short-range transmitter, so monitoring would have to be done close by. If Melman is monitoring, he will probably park somewhere in the vicinity. We could play along with it for the time being, then try to catch Melman in the act of monitoring. Maybe we could bring the Super Trooper along and suggest he be arrested."

"Yeah. Melman probably can't be jailed for eavesdropping, but it would give Bob a good excuse to question him about Richard Vandorn's murder. It might put them off balance and inspire Krupp to do something stupid."

"Yeah, like shoot us."

"There is that possibility."

Next, JB and Charlie inspected the interior of the cabin. Beverly had installed a silent monitoring system with nearly invisible motion detectors in each room. But there were no warnings of intrusion and no other signs that the cabin had been entered.

Back in the car, Charlie called the Super Trooper and asked whether he would be interested in catching an eavesdropper in the act. Bob thought that would be fun and agreed to be on call when they detected that Melman was parked near Beverly's cabin, probably in the late afternoon and evening, when JB and Beverly would plan to be home. Charlie and JB retreated to the *Shearwater*, where they were met by Beverly and Kate as she got off work.

At about four forty-five, the tracking app on JB's phone indicated Melman had left Gertie's Tavern and driven straight to a side road near Beverly's cabin.

"It looks like we're on," Charlie said to Bob, the trooper, on the phone. "Give JB and Beverly about forty-five minutes to get home and settle in. I'll meet you at your office, and we can go hassle Melman."

An hour later, Bob and Charlie were in the trooper vehicle, a new Ford Explorer with a spiffy trooper logo, and were on their way to East End Road.

"Wow, the state is treating you right with this vehicle," commented Charlie.

"Yeah, well, I drove a piece of shit Crown Vic for four years," replied Bob. "I deserved a new ride."

"So, how do you want to handle this?"

"Do you think Melman is prone to violence?"

"I don't think so, although JB and Beverly found a handgun in his cabin. Oops, you're not supposed to know that."

"In the past four years, you guys have broken so many laws in your investigations, it doesn't even register on my radar anymore. But, to answer your question, the best approach is probably to drive right up and surprise him, since we know where he's parked."

"I agree. I'd be very surprised if he puts up a fight."

Charlie received a text from Beverly indicating that they were home and carrying on a "normal" conversation, so Melman should be listening.

The white and blue Explorer pulled onto the side road where Melman was parked and drove up next to him. Bob waited until they were about twenty feet away and turned on the siren. John Melman, who had been wearing headphones, jumped about two feet and hit his head on the roof of the car. The trooper's loudspeaker ordered him to get out of the car and keep his hands visible. He meekly complied.

Bob handcuffed him and told him he was under arrest for illegal eavesdropping and conspiracy to commit a crime. Melman was in total shock that he was actually being arrested. He was transported to the trooper's office and locked in the interrogation/storage room. He complained that his head hurt.

"I think we should see if Michael Vandorn would like to be involved in questioning our master criminal," suggested Charlie. "As a federal prosecutor, he has law enforcement credentials. Also, it would be good if JB and Beverly could listen in."

"Ok. It's probably against procedures, but what the hell."

Charlie called Vandorn, who was excited about maybe getting some information and said he would be right there. JB and Beverly were already on their way. Melman was left to marinate in the interrogation room while the forces gathered.

John Melman was thinking, *Who the hell are these people?* as the interrogation/storage room filled up. The Super Trooper moved boxes of files into the corner so there was room for everyone.

"So, why were you listening to conversations in Beverly's house?" asked Bob.

"Who's Beverly?" Melman said.

"That would be me," replied Beverly with a cute smile.

"I thought a guy named JB lived there."

"And that would be me," replied JB. "In fact, I also live there."

"Oh," said the clueless Melman as he fidgeted in the uncomfortable chair.

"Getting back to the original question, why did you bug the house?" repeated Bob.

"I don't know. I just thought it would be fun."

"Do you know a man named Stanley Krupp?" asked JB.

"I don't think so."

"That's odd since we have a recording of you talking to Mr. Krupp a few weeks ago," JB replied. "We also suspect you met Krupp at the airport this morning and planted the bug."

"Oh, crap," whined Melman.

"What did you guys hope to accomplish?" asked Beverly.

"I don't know. I just do stuff for Stanley once in a while. He pays me for information."

"What kinds of stuff do you do for him?" asked Bob.

"I just keep him up to date on things going on in Homer. I guess I'm sort of a local informant."

"What does Stanley do with this information?" asked JB.

"I don't know that either. Says he wants to make the country better. I guess he and some other government guys have plans, but I don't know what they are."

"Did you murder Richard Vandorn?" asked Michael.

"What? Fuck no. And who the hell are you?"

"I'm Michael Vandorn."

"Oh, shit. I had nothing to do with that."

"Did Stanley Krupp have anything to do with it?" Michael asked.

"I don't think so. In fact, Stanley asked me if I knew who did it. It seemed like he was pissed that so much attention was coming to the area."

"Do you know of anyone else in the Homer area who is working with Krupp?" Bob asked.

"No. But, I think he has fishing buddies in Kenai, so they may be helping him out."

"Ok, Mr. Melman," Bob said. "I'm going to write you up for misdemeanor eavesdropping and let you go. If I find out that you've been hassling these people or have any more communications with Stanley Krupp, you will spend some time in jail. This is a continuing investigation, and Krupp may be involved with some seriously bad stuff, so stay away from him. We'll be watching."

The Super Trooper completed the paperwork for Melman's misdemeanor arrest and let him go. He contemplated trying to get a search warrant for Melman's cabin, but decided it was not worth it since the Mooseketeers had already illegally searched the place. JB and Beverly retreated to their cabin, Michael retreated to his brother's boat, and Charlie retreated to the *Shearwater* to discuss the events of the day with Kate.

Chapter 30

After several frustrating days of trying, Gloria Alvarez finally managed to arrange a private meeting with the Vice President. She insisted that no one else be present and that the meeting take place somewhere away from government buildings. Private is a relative term when it comes to meetings between high-level government officials in Washington, D.C., because of security details and public scrutiny. They decided on a small Italian restaurant away from the Capitol and instructed their security details to maintain a discrete distance.

"So, Mark, what's going on with the conspiracy to remove our bodies from the planet?" Gloria asked.

"Unfortunately, not much," replied the VP. "Not knowing who to trust and skepticism about the plot in general among the few folks I've confided in has led to frustrating inaction."

"Who else have you confided in? Has the president been informed?"

"The president hasn't been informed, at least that I am aware of. In addition to the Secret Service people who were present during the assassination attempt, I've only told the Deputy Attorney General. At least one member of his staff has corresponded with Federal Prosecutor Michael Vandorn, whose brother was killed in Alaska. Mr. Vandorn has evidently been working with the folks from Homer, Alaska, who uncovered the conspiracy and basically saved my life."

"I spoke with Mr. Vandorn, and we agreed to exchange information as it becomes available. What do you think the chances are of federal law enforcement actually going after the conspirators?"

"We seem to be in a bizarre situation where nobody knows who to trust in the FBI or the Secret Service. Consequently, nothing is happening in D.C. I assume that Federal Prosecutors in Seattle are questioning the sniper who was going to shoot me, but I haven't heard diddly about that. I don't even know if they've identified the guy. Alaskan authorities seem to have been kept out of the loop."

"Great! So, our lives are in danger, but nobody wants to take responsibility for investigating. Once again, politics trumps everything."

"I guess that's about it. Do you have any suggestions?"

"I'm not going to just wait around for a sniper to take a shot at me. I'm thinking of going to Alaska and doing my own investigation. That seems to be the only place where anyone knows anything."

"How are you going to do that without creating a massive scandal? Our travel schedules are known to everybody."

"I don't know. I haven't figured that out yet."

Gloria got up and left the restaurant without eating, trailed by her Secret Service watchdogs.

Back in her secure office, Gloria summoned her trusted assistant, Phillip, locked the door, and sat pensively at her desk staring at the wall.

"What have you found out about Stanley Krupp?" asked Gloria.

"There's a folder on your desk with what I've got so far," answered Phillip. "He has an Ivy League education and a law degree. His history after college is a little fuzzy, so I suspect some black ops in his past. In recent years, he has operated an equally fuzzy lobbying group called Gentle Persuasion. He has a known association with Senator Strunk and some of the more radical members of the intelligence community. There are rumors of a cabal of sorts, but no hard information. He divides his time between Washington and Alaska, where he has a cabin in a remote area. He has a pilot's license and flies his own plane."

"Ok, here's what we're going to do," Gloria said as the situation came into focus in her mind. "I need to get to Alaska without anyone knowing about it."

"How the hell are you going to do that?" asked Phillip.

"I'm going to get a bad case of the flu and become bedridden for about a week. You are going to be the only person allowed in my house. The Secret Service guys will be stationed outside. I have a false set of identification papers left over from my CIA days, which no one knows about. My new name will be Stella Martinez. I'll sneak out of the house, catch a cab to the airport, and—voila—I'm gone."

"What if someone recognizes you?"

"I'm new on the job and not that many people are familiar with my face yet. I think I'll be alright with a different hairstyle and glasses."

"What are you going to do when you get there?"

"I'm not completely sure. I'll coordinate with the small group of folks in Homer who uncovered this whole thing. The only thing I know for sure is that someone with juice needs to take control. I'm probably the only one who can do that, not to mention my obvious motivation to avoid getting killed."

"What can I do to help?" asked Phillip.

"You can pick up a burner phone on your way home tonight. I'll give you my new ID and phone info, and you can make reservations for flights to Anchorage and on to Homer, leaving tomorrow morning."

———◆———

Bob Stillwater stared once again at the scantily-clad women on the calendar above his desk in Trooper Headquarters. The arrest of John Melman and his apparent association with Stanley Krupp presented a dilemma. He knew from information relayed to him by Charlie and company that Krupp was likely a bad actor and a dangerous man. He was not sure if he believed Melman that Krupp was not involved in the murder of Richard Vandorn. These guys were his only possible lead into the murder, which he was apparently charged with investigating since the FBI had bailed. Additionally, it was almost certain that Krupp was involved with the plot to assassinate the vice president. Bob was not even supposed to know about the VP plot.

Complicating the situation was the fact that Krupp lived in a remote area and had extreme mobility with his private plane. It was not like Bob could just drop in on Krupp and interview him unless he wanted to rent a helicopter. So, what should his role be? He was not even sure whether he should contact his superiors. Somehow, the Mooseketeers had managed to put him in an impossible situation once again.

Bob decided the best solution was to wait and see.

Chapter 31

Gloria Alvarez stepped off the Twin Otter commuter plane onto the tarmac at the Homer International Airport the following afternoon. Her travels had been uneventful—apparently, no one recognized her.

The view from the plane window during the approach to Homer was spectacular. The snow-capped mountains on the south side of Kachemak Bay were set off by the dark green of the spruce forest and the blue water of the bay. The dramatic profiles of two volcanoes were visible across Cook Inlet. A sparkling glacier twinkled in the sunlight as the plane banked for landing. While the reasons for her being in Alaska were less than optimal, she had to admit it was great to get out of D.C. without the usual fanfare. It was almost fun.

Charlie Skyler was there to meet her per her arrangements with Michael Vandorn. She recognized the tall, handsome Viking immediately from his description. Charlie's presence was a bonus. Gloria, a single, attractive middle-aged woman, was always on the lookout for interesting men. Such men were few and far between in Washington, D.C. Charlie recognized Gloria from her photo despite the fact that she had been instructed to wear Alaska-casual clothing. He was surprised at how attractive she was, even in her semi-disguise. Somehow, he had not pictured a cabinet member as being sexy. Onlookers would probably assume Charlie was picking up a client for his tour business.

The two unlikely companions drove immediately to Beverly's cabin, where JB, Beverly, Michael Vandorn and Kate were waiting. After introductions, Gloria asked for biographies of each group member.

"Wow! You guys are pretty impressive," said Gloria. "It seems weird that I'm talking about matters of national security with citizens from a remote Alaskan community. But, given the dysfunction in D.C., it somehow seems appropriate. So, how did you guys get into this mess?"

"Well, it's a little complicated," said JB. "It all started on a rainy night with an uninvited intruder."

The events of the last few weeks were explained in detail to Gloria. Nothing was omitted despite the illegal nature of some of the activities.

"You guys should be working for the CIA," Gloria quipped. "No, on second thought, it's a good thing you're not. I feel I can trust all of you since I sense no hidden agendas. It seems like everyone in Washington has a hidden agenda."

"Any suggestions where we should go from here?" Charlie asked. "What do you hope to accomplish by meeting with us?"

"Well, the first thing I hope to accomplish is to avoid being assassinated," answered Gloria. "But, beyond that, I felt I needed to get to the source of the information. Everyone in D.C. who is privy to your discoveries is afraid to discuss the situation, and I sense that no action is going to be taken until there is a public assassination. I think the first thing we need to do is somehow deal with Stanley Krupp. I've run into Mr. Krupp before, and he's smart, determined, and generally not a very nice person. Unfortunately, he's friendly with my deputy, who is apparently part of the conspiracy if your information is correct. Can we keep track of his whereabouts?"

"We've discovered he keeps up a Facebook dialogue with his adolescent granddaughter, so we usually know when he's in Alaska as opposed to Washington," answered Kate. "As far as I know, he's currently still in Alaska."

"Unfortunately, he found our listening device in his cabin, but we still have a bug in his henchman's house in Homer," JB answered.

"John Melman is pretty much just an errand boy, but we may get some information from there."

"How hard is it to get to Krupp's cabin?" asked Gloria.

"It takes a whole day of overland travel to get there on the ground and requires an ATV plus some hiking," answered Charlie as he refilled everyone's cups with coffee. "A helicopter is the obvious alternative, but the noise might be an issue. I guess a team could be dropped off outside hearing distance and hike in. Landing a small plane on his sketchy airstrip might be another option, but the passengers would be vulnerable to gunfire. When we searched his cabin, we saw a sizable gun safe, so we should assume he's well armed."

"That brings up the question of what a team would look like, and whose authority they would operate under?" asked Michael Vandorn. "The local state trooper has some idea what's going on, but he probably doesn't have authority to act on his own. The FBI should be involved, but we know that some agents are part of the conspiracy. There would probably be leaks."

"Homeland Security encompasses a whole shitload of agencies, so we might be able to cobble together something, but, again, leaks would be a problem," said Gloria as she got up and paced around the room. "Another question is what would we charge him with?"

"JB's tape recording of the discussions to assassinate the vice president and Homeland Security Secretary certainly provides evidence of a criminal conspiracy," added Michael, putting on his prosecutor's hat. "The powers-that-be in D.C. may be afraid to follow up, but I think my bosses in Seattle would support trying to obtain an arrest warrant. I can ask them to be sure. Once we have a warrant, we could probably use local law enforcement to help enforce it. But, if I talk to West Coast federal prosecutors, Gloria, should I mention you're involved?"

"I think you can mention it, but please make sure they understand that secrecy is important," Gloria said as she topped off her coffee.

"Of course."

"But, getting back to an arrest team—who would that consist of?" asked Charlie.

"Once we have a warrant, the local trooper could be the actual arresting agent," Michael said. "Some of us could accompany him. The legality is probably fuzzy, but JB, Beverly, and Charlie have familiarity with the area of Krupp's cabin, so their involvement is a necessity. Beverly has law enforcement experience as a former DEA agent, and JB apparently also has experience. God knows what that consists of."

"I'm not talking, but it sounds like fun," quipped JB.

"Bob Stillwater, the trooper, has worked with us before, and I think he trusts us," added Charlie.

"What about me?" asked Gloria. "I also have law enforcement experience, and I'm probably senior in terms of authority. The shit would probably hit the fan if folks in Washington heard about it, but I don't care. I came up here to help resolve this whole mess, and I intend to do just that."

"You'll get no argument from us, Madam Secretary," said JB.

"I've worked with the local helicopter pilot before," Charlie said. "I can ask him what he recommends as far as getting all of us to the vicinity of Krupp-ville."

"Well, OK, I guess that's settled," said Kate. "I can provide coordination on the ground and computer assistance. I just checked Krupp's Facebook account. It sounds like he's going to be in Alaska for a couple of weeks, fishing with his buddies on the Kenai River and probably spending nights at his cabin. If we do this, it should probably be soon."

"How about the day after tomorrow?" said the Homeland Security Secretary.

———•———

"I DON'T KNOW WHERE the fuck she is," exclaimed Senator Strunk, speaking on the phone to Stanley Krupp. "She's gone completely off the radar. She was supposedly sick and at home, but my informant in her security detail says she's not there, and she apparently left without telling anyone. It seems obvious that she's in hiding, presumably because of the threats against her. My Secret Service guy is looking for her, but has had no luck so far. Also, I've contracted a hitman who is presumably also looking for her."

"Well, shit," responded Stanley. "That's news to me. Obviously, you've cut me out of your plans. Thanks for the vote of confidence. So, what do we do now? All our names are out there as conspirators, but we have no idea whether anyone is going to follow up on the information. Plus, my attempt to bug the house of one of the Homer busybodies was a complete failure, and my Homer contact has been compromised. Melman says he didn't implicate me when questioned by the trooper, but he's not the sharpest knife in the drawer. I'm half expecting a SWAT team any minute."

"Let's not get dramatic. All of my sources suggest that nothing's going to happen. I have assurances that the FBI is not going to follow up. The crazy tape recording from Alaska is regarded as the product of kooks using artificial intelligence to stir things up. Just stay cool."

Stanley was definitely not cool. He did not know whether his wilderness hideout was an advantage or a disadvantage. On the one hand, it was hard to get to and offered a good defensive position. On the other hand, the assholes from Homer had obviously figured out how to access the cabin without being seen. He removed several guns from his gun safe, loaded them, and placed extra ammo in convenient locations. He was not going to go quietly.

CHAPTER 32

IN THE EARLY MORNING two days later, a motley crew of individuals with extremely diverse backgrounds gathered on the tarmac at Kachemak Choppers. The day was cloudy and calm with oppressive humidity, portending a bad bug day. The owner and principal pilot for Kachemak Choppers, Mike Krezinski, was briefing his passengers on helicopter safety protocols. Mike was one of the few Vietnam-era helicopter pilots still flying. Although in his early seventies, he had flown so many hours that operating a chopper was purely instinctual. His vision and reflexes remained good, and Bob, the trooper, would not fly with anyone else. Alaska's rugged terrain and changeable weather created challenging conditions for flying. Landing in forested terrain offered additional risks. Mike had once misjudged the space between the trees and chopped off the top of a small spruce tree. The creased rotor was in good enough shape to get back to town, but a replacement rotor blade had cost him a cool twenty thousand dollars.

The Bell Jet Ranger helicopter had room for three or four passengers, so it was determined that two trips would be necessary to get the full crew to a staging area within hiking distance of Krupp's cabin. The first load consisted of the Super Trooper, JB, and Beverly. The second load consisted of Charlie, Michael Vandorn, and Gloria Estevez. The seventy-mile round trip from the airport to the staging area required about forty-five minutes at ninety miles per hour.

Two hours later, they were all gathered in a small grassy clearing between two ridges about a mile from Kruppville. Everyone in the informal assault team were armed with an equally diverse array of weapons. Gloria had visited a gun store in Homer the day before and purchased an AR-15 type rifle and a Glock handgun, making her the baddest member of the group. It was amusing to all that the Homeland Security Secretary was wandering around in the Alaska wilderness armed to the teeth. She assured everyone she was a very good shot. No one doubted her. Trooper Bob, Beverly, and Michael carried 9 mm handguns, and Charlie carried a twelve-gauge shotgun. JB carried his beloved .32 caliber Beretta pocket pistol.

Charlie also carried a portable VHF radio to communicate with the helicopter. The pilot suggested that he would stand by on a high point within radio range so that he could respond quickly as needed.

In spite of the seriousness of the mission, Gloria was having a great time. Escaping from the phony rituals of Washington, D.C., was exhilarating. Although the walking was difficult, she was fascinated by the south-central Alaska ecosystem. The hilly terrain featured alternating stretches of muskeg overlain with black spruce and sphagnum hummocks, upland white spruce forests on the higher ground, birch forests on the ridge tops, and small clear streams teaming with salmon. The mosquitoes and flies were bad, but she was prepared for the bugs, having doused herself with repellent. She observed two moose peacefully browsing on shrubs. It was all very different from South Texas, where she had grown up, and even more different from Central Mexico, where she had often visited her aunts and uncles.

Beverly took a phone photo of Gloria in her badass outfit and threatened to send it to the Washington Post. "It might not be a bad idea," Gloria said. "Maybe some of my colleagues in D.C. would take me more seriously."

Charlie led the way using a combination of GPS mapping and his general knowledge of cross-country trekking in Alaska. Walking was difficult at best, and he tried to find the easiest route, avoiding muskeg and thick brush as much as possible. As they approached the final ridge before the cabin, he cautioned everyone to be quiet and carefully eased into a spot where he could view the cabin without being seen.

"He's here," said Charlie, excitedly. "His plane's at the strip. Is everybody ready to do this?"

The impromptu mission suddenly became real, and the tension level increased dramatically. JB and Beverly outlined a plan of attack. Since there was only one door and most of the cabin windows were small, everyone except Charlie would approach from the front. Charlie would approach from the back in case Krupp tried to exit from the somewhat larger bedroom window.

Bob, Gloria, JB, and Beverly spaced themselves along the back slope of a narrow, aspen-covered moraine that curled around one corner of the lake and faced the cabin. JB figured the narrow ridge would serve as a backstop against any flying bullets. With everyone in position, the Super Trooper removed a megaphone from his backpack.

"Stanley Krupp—State Troopers!" shouted Bob. "We have a warrant for your arrest. The cabin is surrounded. Come out with your hands above your head!"

All was quiet for about a minute, then automatic rifle fire raked the area in front of the cabin. Shredded white aspen bark fell like snow, and gravel spit from the ridge top.

"Holy shit!" exclaimed Beverly. "We're already outgunned. Is everyone OK?"

"All good, except for a little sand in the face," said Gloria as she hunkered farther down the ridge.

"I guess this operation is going to require some finesse," remarked JB.

"No kidding," shouted Beverly.

"How about I empty a magazine from my rifle into the cabin?" suggested Gloria. "The thick log walls will probably stop most of the rounds, but it will show him that we mean business."

"Go for it," said Michael.

The silence was shattered for about fifteen seconds, followed by what seemed like a total lack of noise. Bird song and other forest noises were unnaturally absent. But, incongruously, a single mournful cry from the loon on the lake filled the gap, somehow seeming appropriate. The normally sweet smell of summer vegetation was replaced by the smell of cordite. Some of the rounds from Gloria's rifle shattered a front window, and some did considerable damage to the front door. There was no movement from within the cabin.

JB received a text from Charlie asking if everyone was alright. He texted that he was at the back window looking in, but the bedroom door was closed, and he couldn't see through to the front of the cabin.

Michael, who was stationed at a location where he could see a side window, fired several shots from his Glock, breaking the window. More automatic rifle fire followed from the side window toward Michael's position. More aspen bark floated to the ground. Then all was quiet again.

'This is kind of a pointless standoff that could last for a long time," said JB. "I'm going to try to shorten it."

"You're going to be crazy again, aren't you?" replied Beverly.

"Maybe. I'm going to move out of sight and swing around to the right side of the cabin. I may be able to get a shot through the little window on that side. It would obviously be best if we could capture Krupp alive, so I'd like to try for a sublethal shot."

Beverly thought of the Mooseketeers' involvement in law enforcement efforts over the last few years. JB had often risked his life despite the group's objections. The others also thought JB was taking an unnecessary risk. But he had a strong aversion to killing people, a result of his history in unsavory black ops situations—one of the reasons he had changed career to a mild-mannered university professor. He was generally opposed to current law enforcement policies of always shooting to kill. He realized there were situations where officers had no other options, but there were also situations where shooting at center mass was not necessary to resolve a potentially violent situation. Plus, a living criminal possessed more information than a dead one. He thought Stanley Krupp could tell them a lot about the Project Nemesis conspiracy.

JB suggested that Bob give Krupp another opportunity to surrender, but if that did not happen within a few minutes, he would pursue other options. He informed Charlie via text that he should fire his shotgun through the back window toward the bedroom door when he gave the signal that he was in position at the side window. The rest of the group was similarly instructed to fire on command. He began to move through the vegetation out of sight of the cabin, circling around to the side of the structure.

———•———

STANLEY KRUPP WAS SITTING in his easy chair, drinking his third cup of coffee. He had finished breakfast and was scrolling through his email to see what was new in his world of intrigue. To say he was startled by the sudden voice of the state trooper would be an understatement. What the fuck? It took him a few seconds to comprehend that he was totally screwed. Things were not supposed to end this way, and he was determined not to go quietly.

He reached for his modified AR-15, got on the floor and aimed out through a small gun port built into the wall. Without seeing any actual targets, he fired in a sweep across the front yard, using a full magazine in a few seconds. He reloaded and waited to see what would happen. Shortly thereafter, semi-automatic rifle fire tore up some of the more vulnerable parts of the front wall of the cabin. So, he was facing at least one assault rifle, but probably no machine guns. Three shots from a small firearm shattered the side window, indicating at least two people. But how many more were there?

He was pinned down with no way to escape, so he had no choice but to wait it out and hope that he had enough firepower to discourage whoever was threatening him.

———◆———

JB CIRCLED THROUGH THE trees and carefully made his way to the side of the cabin. Peering into the small window, he could see Stanley lying on the floor with his gun facing out toward the rest of the team. He heard Bob announce one more time for Krupp to surrender, followed by no movement from Krupp. JB texted "Go."

The quiet wilderness was shattered by the sound of gunfire from three sides of the cabin. The boom of Charlie's shotgun was especially loud; the large buckshot pellets made gaping holes in the door that separated the bedroom from the front living room. JB took advantage of the noise to break out the glass in the side window, trying to synchronize the glass breaking with the rhythm of shots from outside. Stanley was flat on the floor and did not hear the breaking window. JB rested his hand on the windowsill and carefully aimed his little pistol at Stanley's left knee. JB knew that knee pain was severe and usually incapacitating. The twenty-foot shot was not unduly difficult. Two quick cracks from the small-caliber gun were followed by a scream from Krupp. Two more quick shots in the direction of Stanley's hands caused him to drop the rifle.

The rest of the team moved in as soon as they heard the scream from the cabin and JB's yell that it was safe to approach. Bob shot the lock on the front door and carefully approached the wounded man while JB remained at his post at the window with his gun aimed at Krupp. The rest of the team entered the cabin and stared at Stanley Krupp cowering on the floor, holding his knee. When he saw Gloria Estevez, he was totally shocked. "Holy shit. Madam Secretary. What are you doing here?"

"I figured since you were trying to kill me, I would return the favor," answered Gloria with a smile as she stood over the fallen man, cradling her AR-15 and looking formidable in her recently acquired camo jacket. "I think you may have underestimated some of us."

CHAPTER 33

THE RETRIEVAL OF THE team and their wounded prisoner was relatively uneventful. The helicopter from Kachemak Choppers landed in Krupp's front yard. Stanley received first aid at the scene for his shattered knee and mangled thumb due to flying debris from JB's second barrage. The wounded man was transported to the Homer Hospital, accompanied by Trooper Bob. Bob remained at the hospital to guard the door. Hospital staff were warned to keep quiet about his presence, and phones in the room were strictly prohibited. Stanley Krupp was probably in for several rounds of painful knee surgery before he could be released. It was likely that he would be initially treated in Homer and then transferred to a federal prison hospital facility in Seattle.

Two more helicopter loads were required to relay the remainder of the assault team back to Homer. Stanley Krupp's computer and a briefcase full of documents were retrieved from the cabin and stored at Beverly's cabin until Gloria could return them to Washington. It looked like the data on the computer were encrypted, but Gloria was pretty sure that her staff could decode them.

The very tired group of assault team misfits retired to their respective accommodations to get cleaned up and met later for dinner at Mama's Fish House, which overlooked Kachemak Bay. Kate Perkins, the fourth member of the Mooseketeers, was also present.

"I could get used to this," Gloria said as she gazed out of the big windows at the assortment of water birds frolicking on the bay. "I'm not looking forward to returning to the grind in D.C., especially in view of the current complications."

A waitress returned with a round of strong drinks and took their dinner orders, which mostly consisted of fish and chips.

"So, where do you think things are going to go from here?" asked Charlie.

"I don't know," replied Gloria. "You're the prosecutor, Michael. What do you think?"

"It's a little tricky to say the least. Our office in Seattle is somewhat separate from the main justice department, so I guess we can go ahead and indict Krupp for federal crimes, assuming evidence from his computer corroborates the information on the original tape recording obtained by the Homer contingent. Obviously, the shootout at Krupp Corral will also play a part. I'm pretty sure my boss and other staff lawyers will support such a move. As far as the other members of the conspiracy are concerned, I don't know how that plays out, especially if Senator Strunk and some members of the FBI are part of the conspiracy."

"I would truly love to nail the Senator," replied Gloria. "He is a dangerous man, in addition to being an asshole. I guess I'm the one who will have to build a contingent in D.C. to hold these guys accountable. A lot depends on how much information we can get from Krupp. We should try questioning him tomorrow morning before he has a chance to think too much, and while he is still in pain. I suggested to the doctor that his pain management be minimal."

"Nothing like a little pain to free the mind," quipped JB.

"He's got to know that he's in big trouble, especially if he can be tied directly to the assassination attempt," said Kate. "He may not have much incentive to withhold information at this point."

"Yeah, unless the senator has a major hold on him," added Beverly. "He may also fear for his life."

"I guess we'll find out tomorrow," said Gloria. "Meanwhile, let's enjoy dinner. Tell me about life in Homer."

———•———

THE FOLLOWING MORNING, A crowd of people stood around Stanley Krupp's hospital bed and stared at the wounded man.

"What are the chances of getting a morphine drip so my knee doesn't hurt so fucking much?" groaned Krupp as he winced with every small movement. "I know you guys are intentionally withholding pain meds."

"Let's see how things go," answered Bob.

"Maybe a place to start is for us to tell you what information we have and go from there," said Beverly as she pulled her phone out of her purse and played the recording that she and JB had recorded at Krupp's cabin during the meeting of the conspirators."

"Shit! How did you guys get that?" Krupp said.

"We're very sneaky," answered Beverly.

"Tell us how Project Nemesis came about," said Gloria.

"I can't do that."

"Sure, you can," said Gloria. "At this point, there's no advantage to you to withhold information."

"Except for the minor problem that I'll end up dead. The group includes some very dangerous people."

"We can protect you," said Gloria. "Plus, if you're forthcoming, all the members will be in jail. So, whose idea was the conspiracy to begin with?"

"It's not that simple. I don't even know how the whole idea started. It was sort of a spontaneous thing among various elements within the intelligence and law enforcement communities."

"How did you become the coordinator, or whatever you are?"

"Some of the ex-black ops guys in my consulting company apparently have personal relationships with selected politicians. I think the whole idea originated during various backroom discussions, some of which I may have been involved in. Names were suggested of high-level people who might be sympathetic to a somewhat different approach to government. I was sort of elected to carefully approach some of these people to recruit them into a planning group."

"What role does Senator Strunk play?" asked Gloria.

"He's kind of the unnamed force behind it all. But, at the same time, he's careful to distance himself from any dirty tricks conducted by the group. He sometimes does stuff on his own, which has created some acrimony among the members."

"What kind of stuff?" asked Michael Vandorn. "Did he order the murder of my brother?"

"I honestly don't know for sure, but that seems like a logical conclusion. As far as I know, the members of the group have no knowledge of your brother's murder. We didn't know he was coming to Alaska until he got here."

"That seems sort of strange," said Michael. "We have evidence that my brother had knowledge of some of the senator's unsavory plans, and that he may have secretly come to Homer to help unravel those plans."

"I actually agree with that," replied Krupp. "That was my suspicion as well. For some reason, the senator wanted to handle his breach of security himself. Maybe he was embarrassed."

"Do you have any idea who may have committed the murder?" asked Bob.

"No."

"So, it wasn't the same guy who tried to kill the vice president?" said Gloria.

"Not to my knowledge. I wasn't involved in the arrangements."

"But you were involved in the arrangements leading to the VP's attempted assassination," stated Gloria. "You admitted as much on our taped conversation."

"Yeah," said Krupp as he grimaced in pain. "How about getting me some morphine?"

A knock on the door to Krupp's room was immediately followed by a nurse. "I'm afraid this cozy group is going to have to clear out of here. Mr. Krupp needs to be prepped for surgery."

"Ok. One more question for now," said Gloria after the nurse had left. "How did you contact the sniper?"

"I got his contact information from the dark web. I never learned his name."

"We've got a lot more questions, but we'll leave you be for now," said Gloria as she exited the little room, followed by the rest of the group. "I'll ask the doctor to make you more comfortable."

———◆———

LATER THAT MORNING, TROOPER Bob sat in his dingy office trying to get inspiration once again from the bikini-clad babes on his long-expired wall calendar. He had been relieved of his duty standing guard at the hospital room of Stanley Krupp. Hospital security staff were enlisted and sworn to secrecy. Plus, Krupp's knee was so messed up that escape was highly unlikely.

Bob was thinking that, after all the drama, he was still no closer to finding out who killed Charles Vandorn. He did not know whether it was a local resident or an outside hit man. The fact that the murder occurred in the early morning in a busy harbor suggested that the killer might have been familiar with harbor activity patterns—or maybe not. If he went with the assumption of a local killer, then it seemed likely someone in town knew something. Apparently, the murder of Vandorn was more or less independent of the attempt on the vice president's life, but at the same time somewhat connected. It was all too confusing. He decided to be proactive and actually do some investigating. A good place to start was Gertie's tavern, where a large proportion of Homer's lowlifes congregated.

"Good morning, Gertie," said Bob as he entered the tavern. It was an hour before opening, and Bob knew that Gertie would be alone behind the bar preparing for her busy day.

"Hey, Bob. What can I do to help law enforcement this morning?"

"Do you remember the murder in the harbor back in May?"

As always, Bob tried without success to avoid staring at the tattooed iguana plunging into Gertie's cleavage. Gertie, of course, noticed and smiled seductively. She got a kick out of Bob's embarrassment.

"Sure. What about it?"

"You don't happen to know who done it?"

"Of course not. If I did, I'd tell you."

"I'm just kidding. But I'm sort of at a loss, and it would help me if you caught any vibes from your customers relating to the event. Any people talking about it? Any new shady types that might be suspicious? Anything at all?"

"There was a lot of talk about it right after it happened, of course. Most of the conversation seemed like normal bullshit. I heard that your buddy John Melman got himself in trouble. He was with some of the guys who were joking about the FBI swarm that came and then suddenly left. Any indication that he is involved?"

"He denied being involved, and his gun was not the murder weapon. We don't have any direct evidence to tie him to the crime."

"My intuition tells me that he knows something about it. The way he and his buddies were talking after a few beers seemed a little more than idle chatter. I can't give you anything specific, just a feeling."

"I'd never doubt your intuition, Gertie. You probably have a better handle on the pulse of the Homer underworld than anyone in town."

"Aw, gee. I'm flattered."

Bob headed east out of town and turned into one of Homer's do-it-yourself neighborhoods featuring homes of all different shapes, sizes, and states of construction. John Melman's cabin was at the end of one of the side roads. Bob knew that Melman would be home because Gertie's Tavern wasn't open yet. Melman came to the door as he pulled up to the front door. The front yard, such as it was, featured an abandoned four-wheeler, a very old Toyota Corolla on blocks, and several bags of garbage.

"Whadda'ya want?" asked Melman as Bob got out of his sleek new police four-by-four.

"Have you got time to answer a few questions?"

"No."

"I can see you're busy. I'm going to ask anyway."

Melman slumped down onto the rickety front steps. His dirty T-shirt was emblazoned with the brilliantly humorous slogan, it's hard to find a good piece of ass in Homer. The shirt complemented the camo shorts.

Bob pulled up a broken plastic chair.

"So, what do you know about the murder of Charles Vandorn in the harbor?"

"I thought we've already been through this. I didn't do it."

'I'm not saying you committed the murder, but I think you know something about it. I'm guessing you and your buddies at Gerties have talked about it."

"Everybody's talked about it. That doesn't mean I know anything."

"That's probably true, but think carefully. You're in kind of a vulnerable position. Your boss, Stanley Krupp, has been arrested for attempted murder, and he's talking about stuff. Since you've been his errand boy in Homer, you will likely be implicated in some of his crimes. Any help you can give us will go a long way to making things go better for you."

"Oh, man. Krupp's been arrested? How'd that happen?"

"That's confidential. So, what do you know about the harbor murder?"

Melman closed his eyes, groaned, and burped. He looked up pathetically and said, "Me and the guys were talking about the murder in the harbor right after it happened, and a drunk guy came up to the table and started bragging that he used to be married to the worthless daughter of a bigwig politician. He said he'd done him a big favor and now the guy owed him."

"What'd this guy look like?"

"He had dark skin and a really dark beard."

"What was this guy's name?"

"I only heard his name once. I think it was Polish, something like Koslowski. That's all I know, I swear."

"Ok. Thanks, John. That's a big help."

Back in the office, Bob called Charlie and suggested a meeting among the full Homer anti-conspiracy group, preferably at a secure location. Charlie suggested they meet in the morning on Michael Vandorn's newly acquired boat.

Chapter 34

The following morning in the harbor dawned clear, crisp and cool with a hint of fall in the air. Autumn comes early to south-central Alaska. While most of the lower forty-eight states are suffering from the heat of August, Alaska residents are already planning to wrap up summer activities and get ready for winter.

Kate and Charlie arrived first, boarding the *Wonky* and lounging on the plush settee in the salon while Michael served coffee and pastries. Trooper Bob arrived next, causing a noticeable list as he climbed onto the boat's starboard side. He was followed shortly by JB and Beverly. Gloria, the Homeland Security Secretary, was the last to arrive. She had elected to remain in Homer at least another day to complete the questioning of Stanley Krupp. The spacious cabin on the Nordhavn was comfortable and warm. JB appeared to want to go to sleep.

"So, what's up, Bob?" asked Charlie.

"I got a lead on a possible suspect for the murder of your brother," Bob said as he directed his gaze toward Michael. "Gertie overheard some interesting bar talk between John Melman and his buddies. They were speculating over who might have committed the harbor murder, and one of the guys brought up some rumors of a local man who sometimes engages in such activities. All of which implies that John Melman knew more than he let on when we questioned him. I paid him a surprise visit and suggested he might want to help out in exchange for us looking the other way in relation to his involvement with Stanley Krupp's activities. He reluctantly became more cooperative. Anyway, he and his buddies talked to a guy from Anchor Point who was drunk and bragging that he used to be married to the daughter of a politician. He said that he had just done a really big favor for this big wheel and that the guy owed him. Melman thought his name was something Polish-sounding, like Koslowski. I looked at Anchor Point property records and found a residence owned by a single man named Kaslewsky. I know this is sort of a long shot, but it's all I've got. There's not nearly enough information to get a warrant, but he's definitely a person of interest. I was hoping to get some suggestions from you guys on how to proceed from here. If Kaslewsky is actually our killer, it might be dangerous to approach him. But he could just be a normal citizen."

"If you do pay him a visit, at least one of us should probably go with you," said Michael. "Who is the most qualified to be a bodyguard?"

"I nominate JB," answered Charlie as he poured himself another cup of coffee.

"Gee, thanks, buddy," said JB as he stuffed half a pastry into his mouth. "But it sounds like fun. I accept the assignment."

"How about if I hang back in the trees in case there is trouble," added Beverly.

"Sounds like a reasonable plan," Gloria said. "At least it's better than nothing. I'd sure like to connect Senator Strunk to a hitman. That would definitely make my day. Meanwhile, I was going to review the stuff we got out of Krupp's cabin this afternoon, and then maybe we could take another shot at getting more information from Krupp. Who wants to go with me to the hospital tomorrow morning?"

"I should probably go, since I'm the only actual local law enforcement person in this motley crew," said Bob. "So, are we going to Anchor Point this afternoon?"

"Yeah. Let's meet at your office at one o'clock," suggested Beverly.

———◆———

Anchor Point is a small community about fifteen miles northwest of Homer on Cook Inlet. Residences tend to be widely spaced, and Kaslewsky's cabin was located at the south end, well back in the trees. Bob, JB, and Beverly approached in the well-marked trooper vehicle. The driveway was long and sinuous, assuring total isolation. Beverly got out of the car, out of sight of the cabin, and hiked through the trees for a couple hundred feet until the front door of the well-built frame cabin was visible. She concealed herself behind a large spruce.

As Bob and JB pulled up, a man stepped onto the front porch. Kaslewsky was a large man with broad shoulders who appeared to be very fit. His dark complexion and very dark, full black beard were consistent with the Eastern European heritage suggested by his name. He wore jeans and a flannel shirt and had a semi-automatic handgun in a holster on his belt. The presence of the gun was not altogether unusual in rural Alaska, nor was it illegal, but it did contribute to a somewhat menacing appearance.

"What can I do for law enforcement this morning?" asked the man.

"Are you Mr. Kaslewsky?" asked Bob.

"Yep."

"I'm Trooper Stillwater, and this is my associate, JB Bachman. We're conducting an investigation of a murder that occurred in Homer Harbor a couple of weeks ago."

"I heard about that. But what brings you here? I don't know anything about it."

"We're just following up on a lead. Someone matching your description was seen in the harbor on the morning of the murder. Can you verify your whereabouts on June third?"

"Crap. I don't know. That was a couple weeks ago. Let me think. I was probably either here or out on my boat. Why would I kill someone in Homer?"

"Can anyone attest to your whereabouts on the morning of June third?'

"I don't know. I would have to reconstruct my activities."

"Do you have a calendar or a diary or something that would help you do that?"

"Let me check," said Kaslewsky as he entered the cabin. JB got behind the trooper vehicle as backup in case he re-emerged with gun blazing. Beverly saw what was happening and also readied her gun in case of problems.

———◆———

Jannis Kaslewsky was enjoying a cup of coffee at his kitchen table when he saw the trooper vehicle pull into his yard. What the fuck? The presence of cops at his house was obviously worrisome, given his recent activities. He was sure that he had covered his tracks during his latest job. He was determined to play it cool, since he could not imagine what kind of evidence would point the authorities to him. He went out to meet them, assuming that polite cooperation would assure them he was an upstanding citizen.

But when the trooper started to question him about the Homer harbor murder, it became obvious they had some reason for being there. Even if they had no real evidence, it was unlikely that they would leave him alone for very long. At the very least, his anonymous isolation in Alaska had come to an end. He wished he had never met Senator Strunk's worthless daughter and gotten caught up in the senator's schemes. Unfortunately, the Strunk family had so much dirt on him that he had had no choice but to do as Papa Elmore had asked. As he walked back into the cabin to ostensibly get his appointment calendar, he quickly concluded that the only course of action was to shoot it out and run. It was either now or later. The trooper did not strike him as being very smart, and the dweeby guy with him did not look like a threat. He grabbed his loaded AR-15 and carefully aimed out the open kitchen window.

———◆———

"Gun!" yelled JB as he and Trooper Bob dove behind the vehicle.

JB had noticed that Kaslewsky, while polite, was more nervous than he should have been, given the circumstances. Consequently, he was hyper alert for any indication that Kaslewsky might try to shoot it out. His eyes were glued to the open kitchen window, and he noticed the end of a barrel come into view. Before Kaslewsky could take aim, JB fired at the window with his compact Beretta, sending broken glass into the building. Kaslewsky returned fire with his semi-automatic rifle, but JB and Bob were shielded by the full length of the trooper SUV. Beverly, seeing what was going on, also opened fire in the direction of the window. The gunfire stopped.

"Shit!" said JB as he saw the gun barrel pull back from the window. He ran out from behind the SUV and around to the back of the cabin. Kaslewsky was just emerging from a back door and did not see JB.

"Stay where you are!" yelled JB while taking careful aim at Kaslewsky's lower body.

"Fuck you!" shouted Kaslewsky as he swung the rifle around. JB shot him in the leg, causing the Polish gunman to fall and yell more obscenities. He rolled and tried to get into firing position.

"Hold it right there and throw your guns to the side!" said Bob as he and Beverly turned the corner around the other side of the cabin.

"Ok, ok," answered Kaslewsky. He wisely realized that with three guns pointed at him, things did not look good.

Bob called for an ambulance while Beverly retrieved a towel from the cabin and pressed it against the leg wound. Fortunately for Kaslewsky, the small .32 caliber bullet had not hit the femoral artery.

"Who are you people?" said Kaslewsky as he was being loaded into the ambulance.

"Just concerned citizens," answered JB.

"You put three holes in my new ride," exclaimed Bob while looking at the front of the police Explorer. "I'm not happy."

Chapter 35

"Catching Kaslewsky was an amazing piece of luck," said Charlie to the small group of Homeroids plus a Homeland Security Secretary gathered on the deck of the Shearwater. The sun was shining and the wind was calm. Harbor activity hummed around them. It was the end of the fishing day, and large totes filled with halibut were being hauled from charter boats to cleaning stations at the top of each dock ramp.

"It will be even more amazing if one of our killer's guns proves to be the weapon that killed my brother," said Michael Vandorn. "If that doesn't happen, we have very little evidence that he committed the murder. But, if we can prove he killed Michael, we should have some leverage to get more information out of him."

"Bob couriered all of Kaslewsky's guns to the state crime lab with priority instructions so we should have an answer in a couple of days," said Charlie. "The fact that we found a suppressor for his Glock, plus his willingness to shoot it out with the police, certainly suggests culpability."

"Boy, I hope so," Gloria Estevez said, "The bar conversation that Melman overheard suggests that Kaslewsky may have direct ties to Senator Strunk. If we could prove a relationship, it would definitely make me happy. I've asked my loyal assistant in D.C. to check for any possible connections. He has the resources to look at multiple databases and can probably hack into Kaslewsky's computer, confiscated from the scene."

"Considering where we started from, I think we're making major progress in derailing Project Nemesis," added Beverly as she sipped her beer and basked in the sun of an unusually nice Homer day. "When are you going back to D.C., Gloria?"

"I would love to stay right here. You guys have a pretty good life. Washington is hot, and the politics are a continuous shitshow. But, unfortunately, duty calls. I guess I have a pretty important job, but it's really hard to get anything worthwhile accomplished in a divided and sometimes corrupt political atmosphere. I have reservations to fly back day after tomorrow. I need to take another shot at questioning Krupp before I leave."

"I, for one, am glad you're there," said Kate. "It's nice to know that there is someone courageous in Washington. But, what if the plans for your assassination are already in motion?"

"That's one of the things I hope to find out from Krupp," answered Gloria.

———◆———

At eight-thirty the following morning, Gloria, Michael Vandorn, and Trooper Bob entered Stanley Krupp's hospital room. A morphine drip had been hooked up to his IV, and Stanley looked sleepy and more comfortable than on their last visit. His leg was raised, and his knee looked freshly bandaged.

"What do you guys want now?" mumbled Krupp.

"How did your surgery go?" said Gloria as she approached the bed.

"It hurt like a son-of-a-bitch until they got the morphine hooked up. Thanks for asking," Stanley replied sarcastically.

"So, aside from you and Senator Strunk, who is next in command of your band of merry men?" asked Gloria.

"I don't really feel like talking. You can go fuck yourselves."

"That doesn't seem very cooperative. You might want to consider the fact that you are in a shitload of trouble. You've suggested that your life might be in danger from other members of the group. Since you're going to spend a long time in jail, the type of prison will, in large part, determine how much danger you may face. One option might be one of the safe federal prisons designed for white collar criminals, where inmates reside in relatively plush quarters. But another option might be one of the big federal prisons for violent offenders. Your safety definitely couldn't be assured within the general prison population. I think I could pull some strings to keep you safe if you help us out."

"Crap. There really is no next in command. Most of the guys at the meeting at my cabin are sort of along for the ride, hoping to get positions of power when the dust settles. The person with the most juice is probably Mack Fraser, the Secretary of Defense. He is dangerous and has many contacts in the intelligence community willing to sign on to an alternative government path."

"And what does that alternative path look like?"

"Mostly one with more power at the top of the food chain."

"Where does the current president fit into all this?"

"He doesn't. But Fraser and others have enough dirt on the president to make him come along."

"So, getting rid of the vice president and me was intended to clear the path to blackmail the president."

"Yup."

"What was the plan for my demise?" asked Gloria.

"There wasn't one."

"You're lying. We recovered some communications from your computer suggesting that Senator Strunk instructed you to find a hit man to accelerate my departure from the earth. For obvious reasons, I'm very interested in stopping that effort."

"As far as I know, the senator changed his mind and decided to make the arrangements himself. Anyway, I think it may be too late. Once a contract is initiated, it usually can't be stopped."

"It had better be stopped," exclaimed Gloria. "As far as the guy you hired to kill the Vice President, I'm going to set up a secure link with my cyber analyst in D.C. so that you can describe to him all the steps you took to employ the assassin. He should have your computer by now. With some luck, we may be able to unravel the encryption and get some hint as to the guy's identity."

"Oh, great," said Krupp. "Then I'll have someone else trying to kill me."

"You probably should've thought of that earlier," Michael said.

———◆———

AT THE SAME TIME that Stanley Krupp was being questioned in Homer, the hitman anonymously contracted by one of Senator Strunk's lackeys to assassinate Gloria Estevez was reclining on a plush king-sized bed in one of Washington D.C.'s upscale hotels. Lately, he had been using the name Ben Madison. He was of average height, medium build, with short brown hair. His face was unremarkable. In other words, he was sort of a nondescript human being—a definite advantage in his profession. A few hours earlier, he had received word that the assignment to kill the Homeland Security Secretary was a go. Half of the financial incentive had been wired into his offshore account. He was anxious to complete the job and collect the remainder.

But it seemed that Gloria Estevez was nowhere to be found. She apparently had not been in her office for several days, having called in sick. All attempts to get additional information through government channels had been stonewalled. Pretending to be a Senate staffer, he did manage to speak with her assistant. The assistant's manner clearly indicated that he was covering for her. Ben planned to stake out her home that evening, but he had a bad feeling that she did not want to be found.

After dark, he made several runs past Gloria Estevez's large house in an upscale Virginia suburb and noted that only one light was burning in a downstairs room. It was the kind of neighborhood where strange vehicles would be noted by residents, so he continued on to a small neighborhood shopping center about six blocks from the house, parked, and walked back to the house, keeping in the shadows as much as possible. The landscaping between Gloria's house and the adjoining property was conveniently arranged so that Ben was able to walk unseen between the hedges until he had a view of the back door and patio. Large sliding glass doors provided a view into the kitchen and family area. There was no sign of any activity. Ben decided to hang out for a while since the weather was pleasant, and he had nothing better to do.

Much to Ben's surprise, a car pulled into Gloria Estevez's driveway a half hour later. Through the patio doors, he could see a man enter the front of the house, disarm a security system, turn on a bunch of lights, and move through several rooms. After about ten minutes, the man left, turning out all but the one light on the way out. As far as Ben could determine, it looked like the man was checking mail and messages, as if for someone who was away for a while.

Ok, Ben thought. She's gone away. But where?

It was obvious that the house was now empty. Ben really wanted to get into the house to look for clues as to her whereabouts. But the security system was problematic, the degree of difficulty depending on the sophistication of the system. Ben had seen a camera on the outside over the terrace, but he had not seen any obvious outside motion detectors. Fortunately, it was extremely dark in the back yard, and there was little chance of being seen from nearby houses. He desperately needed more information.

Ben worked his way between shrubs up to the house and skirted close to the wall out of camera view. He noticed a kitchen window was partly open. He looked into the kitchen and did not see any motion detectors. Since the window was already open, the window sensor was obviously not in play. Ben managed to crawl through the small window, ending up on top of the kitchen counter. So far, so good. Light from the front room allowed him to see reasonably well. A small desk in a kitchen alcove seemed like a good place to start his search for any useful information.

Using a penlight, he sorted through various paper items in a wastebasket under the desk. A discarded envelope had Delta Airlines scribbled on it, followed by a flight number. Ben pocketed the envelope. A notepad on the top of the desk was blank, but vague impressions of the note from the previous page remained. This he also pocketed. Nothing else of interest was found on the desk.

The assassin decided that he was pressing his luck. Any further movement within the house was likely to set off the security system, and he was optimistic that the notes he had found would help his search for the Homeland Security Secretary. Ben crawled back out the window and returned to his hotel room to examine his booty from the home invasion.

Employing the well-known primitive investigative technique of using pencil shading to outline the impressions on a piece of paper, Ben was able to make out pieces of a travel schedule. It was too good to be true. A technique he had learned as a kid from reading the Hardy Boys mystery books was paying off. The Delta flight, combined with an Alaska Airlines number, combined with a local airline flight, indicated that Gloria Estevez was likely in Homer, Alaska, of all places. Notably, there was no indication of a return flight.

What the fuck is she doing in Alaska?" thought Ben. Oh, well. I'm getting paid well, and I've always wanted to go to Alaska. Ben made reservations for an impromptu trip north for the next morning, even though he was not sure how he would find the Homeland Security Secretary once he got there, especially since he did not know what name she was currently using. He googled Homer and found that the permanent population was only about six thousand. But it was summer tourist season, and the actual number of people would be much larger. He needed to find out Gloria Estevez's alias if he was going to have any chance of finding her.

Ben had contacts in the illegal hacking community and asked

one of his sources to look at air travel manifests from the designated flights. Ideally, the number of single female travelers corresponding to Gloria's schedule could be narrowed to a reasonable number, giving him some names to look for. His hacker friend called back an hour later. "There's only one name consistent with your criteria—Stella Martinez."

CHAPTER 36

CHARLIE'S PHONE RANG AT eight o'clock Monday morning as he was finishing his second cup of coffee in the pilothouse of the *Shearwater*. Kate had already gone to work, and Charlie was enjoying the peace and quiet until rudely disturbed by his ringing phone.

"Good morning," said Bob, the Super Trooper, with gusto. "I've got news."

"Ok," replied a sleepy Charlie. "What's up?"

"Kaslewsky's gun, the Glock 9 mm with the suppressor, was definitely used to kill Richard Vandorn. So, we've got him cold."

"Excellent," exclaimed Charlie. "You should be proud since you singlehandedly solved the case. Have you notified Michael and Gloria yet?"

"Yeah. Michael's making arrangements to have his northwest prosecutor's office take over the case, and Kaslewsky is probably going to be transferred to Seattle tomorrow for additional interrogation."

"Wow. If he could get tied to Washington, D.C. bigwigs, the shit could hit the fan."

"We can only hope," replied Bob as he hung up.

Charlie was thinking that things were moving surprisingly fast. He was starting to have some hope that Project Nemesis might actually come tumbling down. But there were still some powerful people involved. The Secretary of Defense was a scary guy with a hell of a lot more clout than a few random citizens from Homer, Alaska. And there was still the specter of an assassin on the loose with orders to do away with the Homeland Security Secretary.

A short time later, JB swung onboard with his usual ungainly flourish, accompanied by Beverly and Gloria Estevez, who arrived with much more dignity. JB's T-shirt du jour was another in his Grateful Dead series, consisting of Jerry Garcia jamming in heaven while God and a gaggle of sexy angels rocked in the background.

"You guys are up early," said Charlie.

"We're concerned about Gloria," answered Beverly. "Assuming that the hitman is already looking for her, he could be on his way to Alaska to find her. After the arrest of Krupp, the word is probably out that she's here."

"I can't believe that we're dealing with a third hitman—all within a month's time," remarked Beverly as she poured herself a cup of coffee. "It all seems surreal. Are there really that many assassins looking for work? Is it that easy to find a "dial a killer" website?"

"Apparently so," remarked Charlie. "There must be a recession in the paid killer market."

"It's pretty damned depressing," said Gloria.

———◆———

Wow, this is a cute little airport, thought Ben Madison as he stepped onto the tarmac at Homer International.

Ben was a city boy, having grown up in Brooklyn. Homer was a far cry from his old neighborhood. As a teenager, Ben had apprenticed as a thug for his uncle, a mid-level enforcer for the local crime family. At the age of nineteen, Ben had killed his first person under orders from his uncle. Being an enterprising entrepreneur, Ben realized that he could make a whole lot more money as a killer for hire.

Furthermore, a police crackdown in New York was making it much more likely that he would end up in jail or worse. Consequently, he changed his name and moved away from the influence of his uncle and tawdry organized crime. Coincidentally, there might have been a pending warrant for his arrest.

Ben was smart and had always been pretty good with computers. He became fascinated by the dark web, figuring it was the new wave of technology in modern crime. He soon set himself up with online contacts and began advertising his services. At twenty-one, he viewed himself as a contemporary "Carlos the Jackal." In his twisted mind, this was a romantic ideal. In the four years since leaving Brooklyn, he had executed five contracts and earned half a million dollars. He could not believe his good fortune.

He rented a compact car at the airport, found a hotel room, and began to explore the town. Homer was a larger, more complex place than he had imagined. Ben was seriously worried about how he would find a single individual with only a name and a photo to go on. He naturally figured that bars would be a good place to start. His experience with bartenders suggested they usually knew more about what was going on than anyone else. He figured that a visit by a Homeland Security Secretary would attract attention, especially in a backwater like Homer.

His first stop was a very sleazy-looking bar on the main drag, called Gertie's Tavern. It was four in the afternoon, and there were five beat-up vehicles of various kinds in the gravel parking lot. Pushing open the heavy wooden door, he almost tripped on the rough wood plank flooring. It was pretty much like sleazy pubs everywhere, with a long bar highlighted by dirty neon beer signs and shelves of liquor bottles. A campy mural of a reclining nude was centered over the bar, and standing in front of it was Gertie, who defied description. Like most customers, Ben was transfixed by Bertie's ample frontispiece and the tattooed iguana that plunged into its recesses.

"What can I get you?" said Gertie with a wink and a smile. She, of course, was well aware of her effect on new customers. In fact, she relied on it for repeat business.

"I'll take a Miller Lite," answered Ben as he managed to pry his eyeballs away from Gertie's boobs. "Say, I heard that there have been some Washington big wheels in town."

"I don't know anything about that," responded Gertie as she opened a Miller and handed it to Ben. "They sure haven't come in here. As you can see, my customers don't exactly fall into the big wheel category." Numerous heads turned and glared at Gertie.

"I was just curious," said Ben while sipping his beer. "Thanks, anyway."

Ben relaxed and finished his beer. He thanked Gertie for her help and exited the tavern. As he got into his rental car, a scruffy young man yelled at him. "Wait a second. I overheard your conversation with Gertie. I heard something about the Homeland Security Secretary being in town. There was a rumor of a shootout in the woods that she was involved in."

"A shootout. You're kidding me. Who was shooting?"

"I don't really know much about it. Just that the troopers and others were involved."

"What others?"

"I don't know exactly. Just some guys from town."

"Ok. Thanks."

Now we're getting somewhere, thought Ben. He began to think that hanging out near the trooper's office might be worthwhile. Maybe Gloria Estevez was using the office as a headquarters. At least it might increase his odds of running into his quarry.

———— ✦ ————

Charlie was changing the oil in his boat engine when Gertie's name popped up on his phone. "What's up, Gertie?"

"A guy I've never seen before came into the bar asking about big wheels from D.C. in town. I played dumb and said I didn't know anything about it, which was basically the truth. But I have a sneaking suspicion that you might, so I thought I'd give you a heads up."

"What did this guy look like?"

"He was average height and build, short brown hair, plain face—pretty nondescript actually. But his clothes had the look of a newcomer. Sort of like he was trying to blend in, but didn't quite make it. His jeans and sweatshirt were new and clean, and he had new athletic shoes on. Sparkly clean sneakers are pretty much nonexistent in Homer. He was driving a clean blue Kia compact, probably a rental."

"Thanks a lot, Gertie. This could be very important information."

"Oh, and another thing. After the mystery man left, our friend John Melman took off after him and spoke to him in the parking lot."

"Wow. More good information. I owe you."

"Just don't forget it!" remarked Gertie as she hung up.

As Charlie was wiping the oil off his hands, his phone rang again, this time from the trooper's office.

"Guess who I just got a call from?" said the Super Trooper. "John Melman. He told me he'd talked to a man in Gertie's parking lot who was asking about important people from Washington being in town. Melman said that he played along and mentioned that the Homeland Security Secretary was here. The guy was very interested, so Melman figured he could get some points from law enforcement by letting us know about it."

"That's interesting. I just got a call from Gertie mentioning more or less the same thing."

"Unfortunately, Melman cleverly mentioned to the guy that Gloria Estevez was here, and that there were rumors of a shootout with the troopers."

"Melman seems to be a few cards short of a full deck."

"So, we may well have yet another hitman in town," said Bob.

"Yeah, this is starting to sound like a bad novel," quipped Charlie.

"When is Gloria planning on leaving town?"

"I think tomorrow morning."

"It would be good if we could keep that information from the mystery man and prevent him from following her."

"Gloria is probably pretty safe for now since the assassin, if that's what he is, doesn't know where she is. Unless he stakes out the airport, he won't know when she leaves. But, since he followed her here, he may have access to flight manifests. We should probably have someone at the airport tomorrow morning. We need to get a better idea what this guy looks like. Maybe Gertie could help. Do you have one of those computer face drawing programs?"

"Yep, but I've never used it," answered Bob.

"This might be a good time to try it."

"Ok. I'll see if I can convince Gertie to help out. I'll head over there right now," said Bob as he hung up.

Charlie called Beverly and suggested she put her phone on speaker so that JB and Gloria could also listen. He filled them in on his conversations with Gertie and the Super Trooper.

"Gloria, what time does your plane leave?" asked Beverly.

"Ten-fifteen."

"So, maybe JB and I could stake out the airport, assuming we get a description of our new bad guy in time," suggested Beverly.

"The problem is we don't know whether our assassin guy is going to play sniper or try for a more short-range solution," said JB. "We'll have to cover both possibilities, although I think long range is a better possibility."

"It seems like, if this guy is going to try to shoot me, the most likely possibility is long range in the parking lot of the airport," Gloria said. "That would be his best chance of targeting me when I'm not in a group of people, and it would maximize his chances of getting away."

"I agree," said JB. "So, I guess we're in the same position we were with the vice president. We'll need to catch him before he gets a chance, which means we need to anticipate where he might shoot from."

"All of which means we need to recon the area and find the best sniper location," added Beverly. "But the sniper will need to do the same thing, assuming that he even knows that Gloria is leaving tomorrow."

Beverly pulled up Google Earth on her computer and zoomed in on the imagery of the Homer Airport. "The whole area is pretty flat, so there isn't any obvious high ground to shoot from. There are a couple of hangar buildings west of the parking lot that might make good vantage points, but it would be difficult for a sniper to avoid being seen, especially since airplanes are always coming and going. I don't really see sniping at the airport as a very good option. The road leading into the airport might work better and provide a better chance of escape. But our hitman doesn't have any way of knowing what car Gloria will be driving or even if she will be alone, which she won't be since one of us will be driving her."

"It may well be that the assassin will come to the same conclusion and decide to follow Gloria back to Washington," said Charlie. "Thinking about all this, it may be our best bet to just make it very hard for the bad guy to get access to Gloria. Let her go back home and maybe try to intercept him here before he can follow. Let's assume we can get Gloria on the plane without giving this guy a chance to do his thing. She can hide out of sight in the car until getting to the airport, and then we can surround her, making it impossible for a shooter to get a shot. We can post people in the airport prior to boarding and try to intercept him if he follows. I suppose he could charter a private flight to Anchorage, but he doesn't know we're looking for him, so that seems unlikely."

"I like your thinking, Charlie," replied Gloria. "After I get home, I'll have security protection, which unfortunately has its own problems, but you guys will be out of the picture. I'd like to thank you guys for all you've done for me. It's sort of unbelievable, really. I wish I could take all of you back to D.C. with me."

"The only problem I see with all this is that the possible assassin guy has thus far committed no crime, and our suspicions are conjecture," interjected Michael. "Any attempt to intercept him will have to be outside the law."

"That hasn't really stopped us so far, has it?" added Gloria.

"We'll be nice," said Beverly.

"Uh-huh," said Michael.

Chapter 37

Ben Madison spent the whole day staking out the State Trooper office on the edge of town. There had been no sign of his target, or anyone else, for that matter. While he was sitting in his car, he discovered that he could access the Wi-Fi of a convenient neighbor. He wanted to know whether Gloria Estevez, alias Stella Martinez, had more travel plans. He got a quick response from his hacker pal, thanks to a generous amount of money. Stella was scheduled to leave Homer the following morning. Oh shit, thought Ben. I just got here. At least I know where she'll be tomorrow morning.

At about five o'clock, the trooper left the office and presumably headed home. It had been a wasted day. Ben decided to scope out the airport to see whether it would be reasonable to fulfill his contract there. A drive to the airport and around the parking lot clearly indicated that there were no reasonable locations for a sniper nest that would provide seclusion and the possibility of escape. There was too much activity, and the terrain was mostly flat and treeless. He could, of course, just walk up and shoot the homeland secretary, but escape from such a situation would be nearly impossible.

Ben began to think that his trip to Alaska might not be a total waste if he could follow Gloria Sanchez back to Washington, D.C. At least he would be able to keep track of her locations. He went online and checked into airplane reservations that would allow him to be on the same flights. There were a few seats available, but they were all crappy middle seats. Oh well. He went back to his hotel.

Early that evening, Trooper Bob dropped by the harbor and caught Charlie and Kate on the Shearwater, engaging in happy hour libations as usual. He had been working with Gertie and his computer drawing program to come up with a face for the hitman. Gertie's long experience observing faces over the bar seemed to contribute to her ability to reproduce the subject's facial features. The drawing was somewhat generic but also looked a little bit distinctive. They hoped that combining the overall description provided by Gertie with the computer-generated face would give them enough to go on when screening people at the airport. But it would certainly be possible to make a mistake and corral an innocent citizen. Obviously, that would be embarrassing and would likely warn the real hitman. Charlie and Kate thought it was worth a try.

The next question was figuring out what to do with the guy once he was identified. Bob suggested they could hold him in the Homer jail as a person of interest, get a quick fingerprint check, and hope that the prints came back with a name. Maybe there would even be an outstanding warrant or some past history that would justify their actions. Michael Vandorn was consulted regarding the legal implications. It was all legally questionable, but it seemed like the best way forward. Now, all they had to do was find the right guy.

Charlie briefed JB, Beverly, Michael, and Gloria about their plans. It was agreed that Bob, Charlie, JB, Beverly, and Michael would meet at the airport in the morning, two hours before the scheduled flight. JB and Beverly would station themselves on opposite sides of the parking lot, and the others would be inside the terminal. Kate would drive Gloria to the airport an hour before her flight, where she would check in as a normal passenger. It was suggested to Gloria that she wear a bulletproof vest, but she refused.

All participants in the conspiracy to nab the assassin retired to their respective lodgings and attempted to sleep. The fact that they had no name and only a vague description was somewhat worrisome, to say the least.

———◆———

JB AND BEVERLY ARRIVED at the airport two hours before the flight and assumed their positions. Each had binoculars. At about the same time, Charlie, Michael, and Trooper Bob entered the airport terminal and tried to loiter inconspicuously. Communication was by text. It would have been great if they had earbuds to talk to each other, like the spy movies. But this was a low-budget operation.

After waiting for about forty-five minutes, Beverly texted that a possible suspect had just entered the rental car return lot with a blue Kia and was walking toward the terminal. JB texted that the guy seemed to match all the criteria. Michael watched from a terminal window as the guy approached and agreed with the assessment.

Bob, Charlie and Michael positioned themselves in the hallway leading to the terminal gate. Bob hid behind the entrance to a restroom since he was in uniform.

As the suspected bad guy passed them, Bob stepped out, and Charlie and Michael blocked the hall. The sort-of-legal kidnapping went without a flaw. The suspected assassin was out of commission. Needless to say, the Mooseketeers hoped it was the right guy.

———◆———

BEN MADISON ALSO AROSE early, packed his stuff, checked out of the hotel, and headed for the airport about an hour before the scheduled flight time. He was bummed because he had to dispose of the rifle and handgun he purchased in Homer without getting a chance to use them for their intended purpose. Both had been dumped into Beluga Lake after dark. He probably could have packed the guns as required by the airlines, but he was afraid of the extra scrutiny and paperwork.

He fully intended to check in normally without giving away his interest in his fellow passenger, Gloria Estevez. It should be no problem. His fake ID had worked well in the past, and he did not expect security at the Homer Airport to be especially stringent.

He drove his rental car to the return area, completed the checkout process, walked with his carry-on bag into the terminal, checked the gate assignment, and started toward the gate. Since there were only two gates, it was not too complicated.

As he traversed the hallway to Gate 1, a state trooper came out of nowhere and suggested he accompany him to the station. Ben turned and started to run, but two civilians blocked his way.

"What the hell are you guys doing? What's this about?" screamed Ben.

"You'll find out shortly," Bob said.

He was essentially grabbed by three people, more or less lifted off his feet, whisked out of the terminal in a matter of seconds, thrown into a trooper vehicle, and transported to the small Homer jail.

Ben was trying to figure out what was going on. As far as he knew, nobody knew that he was even in Homer. Plus, he had not actually done anything illegal, at least not recently. But somehow the authorities knew what he was planning. He began to think that he was well and truly fucked.

———◆———

Gloria Sanchez, Homeland Security Secretary, boarded the plane with the rest of the passengers. She was mostly oblivious of the drama in the terminal. A text from Charlie informed her that the presumed bad guy had been detained.

Meanwhile, the assassin was transported to the Homer jail. He claimed that his name was Ben Madison, and he did not know anything about plans to kill someone. The suspect's fingerprints were collected by an automated digital print reader and immediately sent out to be compared with national print databases.

A computer taken from his carry-on bag was express delivered to Washington, D.C. in care of Gloria's assistant. Gloria called him when she reached the Anchorage airport, told him to expect the computer the next day, and emphasized the need to trace the lines of communication between Ben Madison and whoever had initiated the request to remove her from the earth.

CHAPTER 38

Later that afternoon, Ben Madison was left to marinate in the cell at the Homer jail while Trooper Bob awaited word on his fingerprints. At about three o'clock, Bob received an excited call from his boss at State Trooper headquarters in Anchorage. Apparently, "Ben Madison" was really Angelo Cippino, a former member of a minor New York City crime family. He had disappeared from the radar of New York authorities several years ago. The best news was that Angelo had an outstanding warrant as a suspect in a gangland murder.

Bob thought this was great news for several reasons—it provided supporting evidence for his involvement in the assassination plot, there would be no problem keeping Ben/Angelo in jail because of the old warrant, and his past crimes could provide leverage to get more information about the plot to kill the Homeland Security Secretary.

With all this in mind, Bob, Michael Vandorn, and Beverly sat down with Cippino in a bleak interview room at the jail. The city-run facility was most often used to detain drunks involved in stupid bar altercations and smelled like one might expect.

"This place really sucks," said Beverly as she held her nose.

"That's why my office is on the edge of town," replied Bob.

"What the fuck am I doing here?" whined the hitman. "I was just getting on an airplane."

"We think there might be more to it than that," said Bob. "First of all, we know that your real name is Angelo Cippino and that you are wanted in New York for possible involvement in a murder. We suspect that you were contracted to assassinate the Homeland Security Secretary, and that you followed her to Homer."

"Then why was I planning to leave Homer?" asked Angelo. "I was just here for a visit. Homer is a cool place."

"Because your target was also leaving on the same plane," Michael Vandorn added. "You weren't able to find her in Homer, but you found out that she was leaving, so you were going to follow her back to Washington."

"Who the hell are you?" asked Angelo.

"My name is Michael Vandorn, and I'm a federal prosecutor. You might want to think about your situation. At a minimum, you'll be sent back to New York. Luckily for you, you weren't able to fulfill your contract, so we might be able to work out something on the conspiracy charges if you can tell us who hired you."

"I have no idea. If you're a Fed, you probably know that such contracts are usually handled anonymously through third parties."

"Assuming you're telling the truth, you obviously contacted someone—probably a broker on the dark web," said Michael. "Your computer is on its way to Washington right now and will be examined by a hacker from the Homeland Security Department. Those guys are the best in the world, so we will probably find out eventually. You could save us some time by letting us know which site you contacted."

"Maybe," replied Angelo. "But those sites are protected by so many layers of security that it may be impossible to get information."

"How about if you tell us the name of the site, and let us worry about the encryption?"

"I'm almost embarrassed to tell you. Believe it or not, the name was Assassinations 'R' Us."

"You've got to be kidding," said Beverly.

"I'm really not," sighed Angelo.

"Ok. If that's true, it will help us get started," Michael said. "If you're feeding us a load of shit, we'll find out soon enough."

———◦———

Gloria Estevez was very relieved to get on the plane in Homer without any visible drama. She was even more relieved when she received the text from Charlie informing her they had jailed the probable assassin, and the assassin's computer was being couriered directly to her office. The remainder of her journey went smoothly, although one man on the flight from Seattle to Washington, D.C. recognized her. But she did not care.

While waiting to change planes in Anchorage, she notified her trusted assistant that she would return that evening. She also told him to expect a formidable hacking job involving two computers, one from Stanley Krupp that she was personally carrying and another from a probable hitman who had been stalking her in Homer. The latter would be delivered by courier. He was pretty amazed to say the least. Arrangements were made for her normal security detail to meet her at her house after her return.

When she pulled up in front of her home in an unescorted taxi at eleven-thirty, her head of security met her at the door. He was uncharacteristically angry. "Where the fuck have you been?"

"I've been on a private trip."

"We can't do our job if you sneak away. Things aren't supposed to work that way."

"So, deal with it," said the Secretary as she entered through her front door. "It's late. We can talk about it in the morning."

The secret service guy stomped back out to the street and entered a black SUV, his home away from home when on duty. Gloria passed through the dark, cold house into the kitchen and poured herself a large scotch. Her home felt empty after her week with the group from Homer. In a sense, they were the closest thing to family she had had in a long time.

Although tired from travelling, Gloria was too wired to sleep, so she began to look through some of the documents that had been retrieved from Stanley Krupp's cabin. One of the documents was the Project Nemesis manifesto, which she had already seen. But having an original copy in hand could come in handy. Most of the other documents were printouts of correspondence from various conspiracy members discussing the Alaska meeting and suggestions for fishing excursions. The names of most of the conspiracy members were already known, thanks to snooping by the Homer contingent. Gloria was disappointed with the lack of new information. But one of the last pieces of paper she looked at was an email from Senator Elmore Strunk to Stanley Krupp. Finally, thought Gloria. A direct reference to the Senator.

The email discussed the coordination of the conspiracy and referenced the August 5th Alaska meeting. It was first-hand information implicating the senator. *We've got you, you asshole*, thought Gloria as she broke out into a wide grin. The Homeland Security Secretary put the documents and Krupp's computer into her well-hidden home safe, poured herself another scotch, and went to bed feeling somewhat better about things. All-in-all, her trip to Alaska had been a success.

CHAPTER 39

THE NEXT MORNING, GLORIA went to her office, accompanied by her security detail, like any normal day at the office. She cheerfully greeted her colleagues and her secretary, then locked herself in her large, comfortable office with her assistant, Phillip. She gave strict orders that she was not to be disturbed. The computer formerly owned by Stanley Krupp was handed off to Phillip with instructions to let her know as soon as he found anything interesting. Phillip's office adjoined Gloria's and was similarly isolated from the rest of the building. As a master hacker, his equipment included a variety of devices and software to deal with encryption, not to mention the full resources of the federal government. At about eleven o'clock, the computer confiscated from Ben Madison was hand-delivered to Gloria's office and handed off to Phillip. He went to work.

Meanwhile, Gloria tried to develop a plan for bringing the conspirators to justice. The vice president was obviously on her side, but he was notoriously averse to political backlash. Gloria hoped that the fact that the bad guys tried to kill him might piss him off enough so that he would acquire some backbone. She still had no idea where the president stood in relation to Project Nemesis. She was not even sure if he knew about it. Information from the tape of the Alaska meeting indicated that the conspirators had some kind of compromising information on the president. So, his cooperation was in doubt. Working through the Justice Department and the FBI might be the best bet. But it was also known that at least one high-ranking member of the FBI was involved.

She called Michael Vandorn, who was still in Homer, and conferred with him regarding the best way forward. He suggested that JB's contact in the intelligence community might be able to help put together a team of trusted people to pursue prosecution of the conspirators. Michael agreed to ask JB if he would talk to his intelligence contact. Gloria promised to keep him up to date regarding information gleaned from the computers and told him that there was at least some information implicating Senator Strunk.

Later that morning, Phillip excitedly rushed into Gloria's office.

"I think Strunk's goose is cooked."

"Why? What have you got?"

"First of all, there are several email strings where the esteemed senator confers with Stanley Krupp regarding the Project Nemesis plans, showing his direct involvement. But, more importantly, I may have found a link between the senator, Stanley Krupp and a dark web hitman site. Additional investigation may be required to prove an actual link to the murder-for-hire plots, but it looks pretty damning."

"Wow! That's great, Phillip. Where do we go from here?"

"I may need to bring in an analyst from the FBI who has been investigating dark web stuff for a long time. I guess there is some risk, but I think he can be trusted. The levels of encryption are pretty formidable, but if we can tie down the whole chain of events that led to the assassin following you to Alaska, then we'll be in good shape."

"Ok. Do what you need to do, but be very careful. Limit your conversations to secure locations."

"Yeah. I already figured that. Fortunately, the analyst is a friend of mine. It shouldn't look too suspicious if we go out to lunch together. I'll let you know what happens."

"Thanks, Philip."

———◆———

Once again, JB contacted Karl, his former boss in a previous life and reclusive conduit to Washington, D.C. intelligence back channels. JB brought Karl up to date regarding all the dramatic Homer shenanigans and the unconsummated plot to kill the Homeland Security Secretary.

"Holy shit, Johann. How do you get yourself into this stuff? How can I help?" said Karl.

"Gloria Estevez is trying to put together a group of trusted officials to prosecute all the guilty parties, including Senator Strunk and the Secretary of Defense. Needless to say, she needs to proceed carefully. The vice president would be included in the group as the highest-ranking official. I guess some trusted Justice Department and FBI folks would have to lead the investigation. It's not known whether the president should be included. I've been asked to consult with you as far as who would be the most trustworthy persons for such a task."

"Boy, you're not asking for much. I have a friend who is the Associate Deputy Director of the FBI. I'm positive he is not a part of the conspiracy. I'll talk to him tonight and see what he suggests as a way forward."

"Thanks, Karl. I'll forward the number for Gloria Estevez's private burner phone so you can contact her directly. I'm sure she'll be happy to have someone else on her side."

"Take care, Johann. These are dangerous people."

———◆———

Gloria was reading through the correspondence taken from Stanley Krupp's cabin for the second time when her burner phone rang in her purse.

"This is Gloria. Who is this?"

"Good morning, Madam Secretary. This is Karl, JB's friend. JB and I discussed possible ways forward in your somewhat unusual situation. With your permission, I'd like to contact a trusted friend who is the Associate Deputy Director of the FBI. I think he might be in a position to help coordinate some sort of action against the conspirators of Project Nemesis. You may know him—George Schuler. I've known him for thirty years and I'm positive he can be trusted."

"Yeah. I know George. He seems like a good guy."

"The ideal thing would be to set up a meeting between you, George, and the vice president. But I'm not sure how we could do that secretly."

"Unfortunately, I'm almost certain that my secret service detail is compromised. Part of Taylor's detail may also be in on the plot, although he has confided in Ralph Neff, the head of the detail. Neff should probably also be included in a meeting."

"Maybe one way to assure confidentiality would be to openly meet in Schuler's office on a false pretense. Sort of confidentiality in plain sight. If we meet outside or in a restaurant, everyone would know that something is going on."

"That sounds like as good an idea as any. Once things are set in motion, it will be out in the open anyway."

"Ok. I'll talk to George and see if he can come up with some ideas that might justify such a meeting. Meanwhile, how are you doing after your exciting Alaska experiences?"

"I'm doing well. I'm especially glad to still be alive. In some ways, getting out in the field and actually doing law enforcement work felt good and was a pleasant break from D.C. craziness."

"I understand. Take care, Madam Secretary."

Chapter 40

MICHAEL VANDORN FELT UNSETTLED the morning after Gloria Sanchez returned to Washington, D.C. He sat on a wooden bench on the boardwalk overlooking Homer Harbor. The discussions with Charlie and the gang, while encouraging, still left them with a major loose end—bringing the remaining conspirators to justice. He needed to decompress and consider his options. He cradled a hot double espresso to warm his hands in the cool morning air. Although it was only eight o'clock, the sun was rising in the eastern sky, creating the pink hue of alpenglow on the mountains across the bay. Sunlight glinting off Grewingk Glacier was so bright it was almost painful to look at. It was low tide, and his perch at the rim of the harbor basin overlooked the boats below, providing a clear view. The extreme tidal range in Kachemak Bay caused the floating piers to go up and down as much as twenty-eight feet over the course of a day, like a slow-motion bungee jumper.

The interesting activities occurring below him were a welcome distraction from the disturbing dilemmas presented by Project Nemesis. Unlike many harbors in the lower forty-eight that often segregate work boats from recreational craft, Homer Harbor was more egalitarian. Boat slips contained a random mixture of commercial fishing boats, charter boats, sailboats, skuzzy live-aboards, glossy white fiberglass yachts, and miscellaneous smaller recreational craft. Michael watched as a diverse group of harbor people scurried among the boats occupied by various harbor activities.

At one end of the basin, halibut were being hoisted from the holds of fifty-foot boats to the top of a pile-supported dock, where they would begin their journey through a fish processing facility. At the other end of the harbor, weekend boaters loaded their families onto smaller boats for family excursions. Large numbers of tourists wandered around gawking at all the strange harbor denizens in their knee-length Xtratuf rubber boots, dirty jeans, and yellow slickers. Michael also noticed that quite a few people were gathered around his newly acquired boat, the *Wonky*, looking through the windows and being generally curious about the unusually fancy boat he had inherited from his recently deceased brother. The yacht stood out because of its unusual design and obvious luxury.

His reverie was broken when thoughts of his murdered brother intruded. How was his murder connected to the broader conspiracy uncovered by his new Homer friends? What should he do now? He had already done his part by notifying his boss in the Seattle prosecutor's office, who had, in turn, notified the powers-that-be about the Alaska assassination plans, reaching all the way to the vice president. He was surprised that no one had contacted him—the silence was deafening. He was sure the same was true for Charlie, JB, Beverly, and Kate. They had, after all, uncovered the whole affair and gathered the critical information regarding the conspiracy participants. What the heck was going on?

He was thinking he would go back to the boat and open one of his brother's bottles of expensive wine. As he rose from the bench, he glanced toward the *Wonky* and noticed another person peering into the windows. His manner looked more deliberate and less casual than the other looky-loos. The man was wearing city clothes, and it just seemed like there was something suspicious. He was much too far away to see his face clearly. Michael took a photo with his camera, but was skeptical that the digital image could be enlarged enough to make out his facial features. He decided to follow the guy. Maybe it was paranoia, but what the heck.

Michael watched the mystery man climb the harbor ramp north of his location and walk to a sparkly clean sedan, probably a rental. Michael ran to his car and was able to get on the road in time to keep him in sight, although his quarry had a quarter-mile head start. Fortunately, in Homer, there were not a lot of road options, so following was not much of a problem. He watched the sedan park in front of a tavern on Pioneer Avenue, and its occupant enter the nearly empty establishment. Michael, struck by a sudden craving for a beer, entered the somewhat sleazy joint, and sat at the bar as far from the mystery man as possible. He surreptitiously photographed the man with his camera as he walked by. About a minute later, another man entered and joined the mystery man at a back table. Michael recognized the newcomer as John Melman from the interview in the State Trooper's office. Well, well, thought Michael as he turned away so that Melman would not recognize him. The two men spoke quietly, and their conversation was inaudible.

After finishing his beer, Michael left the bar, careful to keep his back to the suspicious pair, and waited in his car. While waiting, he sent the photo of the mystery man to Charlie. Michael continued to wait until the two men emerged from the bar, going in separate directions. This time, he was able to get a clear shot of the man's face with his phone. He elected to continue following the distinctive rental car, but the surveillance ended at the Best Western Hotel—not very interesting.

Michael returned to the harbor and stopped at the Shearwater to talk to Charlie, who was busy dealing with inquiries for his tourism business.

"It looks like there might be another loose end in Homer," said Michael as he accepted a beer from the galley refrigerator. "I just followed a guy who was scoping out my boat and saw him meet up with Melman. I have an uneasy feeling about the meeting." Michael showed the photo to Charlie, but Charlie had never seen him before.

"Probably we should question Melman again," said Charlie as he phoned the Super Trooper.

———◆———

"What'd I do now?" whined John Melman as he opened his cabin door and faced the Super Trooper, Charlie and Michael Vandorn.

"We're not sure if you've done anything," said Bob. "Can we come in?"

"Do I have a choice?" Melman said as he stepped aside. "There's no place to sit, so you'll have to stand."

The group looked around the bare-bones cabin and wondered how a human being could live in such squalor. The floor was cluttered with pizza boxes, beer cans, and dirty underwear. A musty aroma oozed from its confines.

"This morning you met a man in the Mainstreet Tavern," Michael said. "Who was he?"

"I don't know what you're talking about."

"This guy," said Michael as he showed Melman the photo on his phone of the two men talking at a table in the bar.

"Oh, that guy. Believe it or not, I don't know who the fuck he is. He somehow got my phone number and called me. He told me to meet him or else I'd regret it. He never told me his name."

"Ok. And what did you talk about?' asked Bob.

"He said if I told anyone about the conversation, he would kill me."

"And I thought we were starting to get along so well, John," replied Bob. "If you don't tell us, we'll put you in jail."

"That's just great. I have a choice between death or jail. Jail is sort of winning out."

"Look, we can protect you," said Michael. "If the discussion was that serious, then it seems likely that someone may be in danger besides you. You need to let us know what's going on."

"You guys seem to be attracting killers to Homer," remarked

Melman. "He was basically asking about JB and you, Mr. Vandorn. He said he was with the government and needed to talk to you about national security. But I didn't really believe him. He was pretty angry, and I think he wants you out of the way because you're messing up someone's plans. He wanted to know where you live."

"Did you tell him?" asked Charlie.

"I tried to be as vague as possible without him getting too pissed off."

"Exactly what does that mean?" asked Charlie.

"I may have sort of suggested that the harbor would be a good place to start."

"Great. Did you tell him where JB and Beverly live?"

"No. I said I didn't know."

"Ok. What more can you tell us?" said Bob. "Anything unusual about the guy?"

"He was a big, tough, obnoxious asshole. He might have been ex-military because of his short hair and an M-16 rifle tattoo on his arm."

"Thanks for your reluctant cooperation," said Bob as he moved toward the door. "I suggest you barricade yourself in here until things settle down."

"Or, alternatively, you could hang out at Gertie's," added Charlie. "I doubt whether you would be in danger in the tavern, at least not from this guy."

"I may just do that," said John Melman as he watched his visitors drive off.

———•———

SENATOR ELMORE STRUNK WAS perched behind the big mahogany desk in his spacious Senate office. Behind him was a picture window overlooking some of Washington, D.C.'s iconic buildings. The ego-wall to his left contained numerous photos of his macho exploits around the world, plus photo-ops with assorted well-known politicians and celebrities. A bull moose head was mounted above the office entry door. His ever-present glass of scotch on the rocks was within easy reach.

The senator was angry in the extreme. It was obvious that the wheels were coming off the bus, all thanks to the bunch of busy-bodies in Homer, Alaska—a place where he had never been and never heard of until the current disaster. Feedback from his various sources had notified him that Gloria Estevez, of all people, had helped capture Stanley Krupp. To make matters worse, the Homeland Security Secretary was back in her D.C. office, suggesting that the assassin he had dispatched had somehow failed. He had no idea where the hit-man was now, but he feared that he might have been captured. He did not think that the assassin could be traced to him, but he was not really sure. He was not an expert in cybersecurity.

He was having trouble dealing with the fact that his career as a power broker in Washington politics might be over. All he could think about was revenge against those who had thwarted his ambitions. A part of his brain knew it was stupid, but he could not let it go. The night before, he had dispatched his fixer, Nate Bacchus, to Homer to "take care of things." Nate was totally dedicated to the senator, and vice versa, because of circumstances in their pasts. They had so much dirt on each other that they were forever wed in conspiracy. Nate was the best and most ruthless intelligence agent that the senator had ever known. Senator Strunk's research on Johann Sebastian Bachman suggested that it would take someone like Nate to tackle the annoying man from Homer. Nate's mission in Alaska was simple—remove Bachman, Vandorn and anyone else involved in the Homer resistance from the equation. He figured there would be serious blowback, but he did not care. He was probably at the end of the road anyway.

———◆———

IN THE LATE AFTERNOON, JB was sitting in his comfy recliner reading a mystery novel when his phone rang, showing an unlisted number. He reluctantly answered.

"Good afternoon, Johann," said Karl, JB's former boss and mentor in Washington, D.C.

"Holy cow," answered JB. "You've never called me before. This must be important."

"Yes, it is," replied Karl. "I just heard through the intelligence grapevine that Senator Strunk has dispatched a very dangerous man to deal with you and your friends. His most recent name was Nate Bacchus, but I don't know whether he still uses it. He is extremely good at what he does, and, most importantly, he's a psychopath with no conscience."

"Thanks for the heads up. Interestingly, we just today uncovered his presence in Homer. Michael Vandorn noticed him nosing around his boat and followed him, so we have a photo."

"Please be careful up there. You guys have been lucky so far in your adventures. But Bacchus is much more skilled than the bozos that your informal team has dealt with to date. Be aware that he has the same skill set as you have, plus a lot more recent experience with violent activities. He has no off switch and will pursue it to the end. I strongly suggest you get your friends out of town—and soon."

"I'm sincerely touched by your concern. You must be getting maudlin in your old age."

"Yeah, well, retirement has given me much time to reflect on my past actions. I'm proud that you decided to pursue other things. Please be careful up there."

The line went dead.

———◆———

So, yet another meeting of the Mooseketeers-plus-one was in progress at Beverly's cabin an hour after Karl's call. JB related the substance of his conversation with his old boss. The general consensus was that at least some of them were in immediate danger.

"So, who sent this guy?" asked Kate. "Krupp's in jail and the other guys involved in the conspiracy must know they're about to be in trouble."

"If the mysterious Karl is correct, then Senator Strunk is behind it," replied Michael Vandorn. "All the indications are that he is a vengeful person. Plus, he likely has access to black ops intelligence guys."

"Now what?" said Kate. "We can't just sit around and wait until members of our group get picked off."

"If Melman was telling the truth, he probably doesn't know where Beverly and I live," replied JB as he removed a beer from the refrigerator. "He may not even know what we look like. But he does know about Michael's boat, so I think we concentrate on the harbor for now. We know what he looks like, so we may have an advantage. We need to draw him out somehow, but he is probably very skilled in his chosen profession. He may be watching us right now."

"On that cheerful note, what do you suggest, 'o' wise one?" asked Beverly.

"The safest path would be for some of us to get out of town, maybe on Charlie's boat," JB said. "I'm thinking that Charlie, Kate and Michael should get out of Homer, probably tonight. Michael may well be a primary target because of his role as a prosecutor. Beverly and I can stay here and work with Trooper Bob to try and stop this guy."

"I guess I reluctantly agree," replied Charlie. "We would be pretty safe in the boat since it would be impossible to sneak up on us. But I don't like leaving you and Beverly without backup."

"We'll be ok. I'm guessing that he is going to put a watch on the harbor to see who comes and goes to the *Wonky*," replied JB. "Beverly and I can watch for the watcher."

"What if he sets up at a high point and shoots down into the harbor?" asked Charlie.

"I guess that's possible, but if you guys aren't here, there will be nothing to shoot at. Plus, the harbor is very congested at this time of the year, making it a pretty risky endeavor. If our mystery man's background is anything like mine, I suspect he will likely go with stealth mode—an attack at short range at a carefully selected location. We will need to out-stealth him."

Michael, Kate and Charlie decided to leave immediately, going directly to the *Shearwater*. Michael did not even stop at the *Wonky* for personal items, hoping Charlie had enough clothing to get by. The Shearwater steamed out of the harbor, heading westward into the fading daylight toward an undisclosed destination.

CHAPTER 41

THE FOLLOWING DAY, VICE President Taylor, Gloria Sanchez, and George Schuler, Assistant Deputy Secretary of the FBI, met in George's office. The meeting was ostensibly concerning an immigration issue. The gaggle of Secret Service agents accompanying Gloria and the VP waited outside the office and ogled Schuler's very attractive administrative assistant. Gloria and the VP sat on a comfortable couch with a coffee serving on the table in front of them, while Schuler remained at his desk.

"OK. So, what's going on?" asked the FBI man.

"We have a very serious and unprecedented situation, and we need your help," replied Gloria as she proceeded to fill Schuler in on the plans of Project Nemesis and the incidents that had occurred in Alaska. She placed a copy of the Project Nemesis manifesto on Schuler's desk, played the taped discussion from Stanley Krupp's cabin, and showed photos of the group members who had met up there. A folder of relevant email and text correspondence between Stanley Krupp and Senator Strunk, as well as evidence of dark web communications with murder-for-hire sites, was also shown to the Deputy Secretary.

"Holy shit," said the FBI agent after he had a chance to review the materials. "How come I haven't heard anything about this?"

"The problem we have encountered all along is that we don't know who to trust," answered the VP. "We know that at least one high-ranking member of the FBI is involved. We've tried to keep things under wraps until we can come up with a plan to prosecute these guys. The president knows something's going on, but he doesn't know the details. Do you have any ideas on how we can proceed? Do you think the Attorney General is compromised?"

"While your revelations are kind of out there, I can't say that I'm totally surprised," answered Schuler. "I've had suspicions about the Deputy Director of the FBI for some time, but I think we can trust the director. I also think that the Attorney General will have to respect the amazing evidence that you have presented. While he is politically wishy-washy, he will have to take some action. I can meet with the Director this afternoon and see what he suggests."

"That would be great," said Gloria. "Actually, the sooner this information becomes public, the sooner danger to those of us in the know will dissipate, at least hopefully. But some push back, possibly violent, from Senator Strunk is a possibility that we can't ignore. I'll give you the number from a burner phone that few people know about so that you can keep us apprised as to what is going on."

"This whole thing is fucking amazing," commented the FBI agent as Gloria Estevez and Mark Taylor exited the office.

———◆———

SENATOR STRUNK'S FIXER AND all-around violent handyman, Nate Bacchus, was starting to narrow things down. He knew where Michael Vandorn's boat was located. He had tried to find an address for Johann Bachman but was unsuccessful. These were the two individuals that the senator wanted out of the way as soon as possible. He had been warned that Bachman was a former member of the off-the-books intelligence community and had skills comparable to his own.

Bacchus looked pretty much like what he was. He was just over six feet, lean and muscular, with brown butch cut hair, dark eyes, and a tanned, rugged, and somewhat scary face. He tended to wear tight black T-shirts that emphasized his biceps and pecs. Most people would have pegged him as ex-military.

He was sitting in his rented SUV in the harbor parking lot with a clear view of the *Wonky*. He planned to stake out the boat for a day to see what happened. If there was no activity then he would attempt to locate Bachman. He regretted that he had neglected to ask John Melman about Bachman's location during the earlier meeting at the tavern. Another meeting was probably in order, but Melman was only marginally cooperative. More persuasion might be required.

He watched the fancy yacht until dark and called it a day. He returned to his sketchy hotel room. He was jet-lagged and needed to sleep.

———◆———

GEORGE SCHULER MANAGED TO convince the FBI Director to meet with him almost immediately after hearing about the revelations concerning Project Nemesis.

"So, what's the big emergency?" Director John Christianson said. "I'm kind of busy."

"I think you're going to want to hear this," said Schuler. He described his meeting with the VP and Gloria Sanchez, played the recording from Krupp's cabin, and outlined the other evidence relating to the plot.

"Wow," exclaimed Christianson as he picked up the phone and called the Attorney General's office. He told the AG's secretary he needed to meet confidentially with the AG as soon as possible. A meeting in Schuler's office was arranged for some time in the next hour, or as soon as the AG could get there. The purpose of the meeting was not disclosed.

Randal Howard, Attorney General of the United States, arrived in a state of agitation. Once again, Assistant Deputy Secretary Schuler went through the revelations uncovered by the unlikely group of citizens in Homer, Alaska and Gloria Sanchez's staff.

"What the fuck am I supposed to do with this information?" yelled the AG. "Senator Strunk is one of the most powerful people in town. Does the president know about this?"

"He knows something is going on, but he doesn't know the details." Replied Schuler.

"We need to arrest these guys as quickly and as quietly as possible," said Christianson. His calm demeanor was in sharp contrast to the AG. "I know this is politically inconvenient, but we don't have any choice. There have been attempted assassinations on the Vice President and the Homeland Security Secretary."

"Yeah, yeah," said a somewhat calmer Attorney General. "But the president needs to be read in on what we are doing."

"I agree," replied the FBI Director. "Can you set that up, Randall?"

"I'll try to arrange for a confidential meeting tonight in the White House. Meanwhile, can you guys put together some kind of a plan to execute a mass arrest, hopefully without anyone knowing about it?"

The AG left the meeting with a flourish. The two FBI officials were left thinking about how they could possibly arrest multiple people simultaneously without anyone knowing about it. They were well aware that there are no secrets in Washington, D.C.

Chapter 42

On the morning of the following day, JB gazed out of the big windows overlooking the harbor from inside the small shop of South Peninsula Radar. JB's friend, Raul, was sitting at his workbench, tinkering with the guts of a marine radio.

"So, whatchu gonna do with your old sailboat?" asked Raul. "It looks pretty lonely sitting there without any personal attention."

JB's thirty-two-foot sailboat, *Otterly Ridiculous*, was once a high-quality craft. He had sailed it from Southern California to Homer after being ignominiously fired from his professorial job. The journey had not been easy, and JB had had his fill of open-ocean sailing. The *Otterly Ridiculous* had not budged from its slip in the Homer harbor since he had arrived five years earlier.

"I don't know," said JB. "Probably sell it."

"It's in kinda bad shape. Maybe you should have someone fix it up. You could get your money back when it came time to sell."

"The only flaw with that plan is that I'd need money to begin with to repair it. Beverly would kill me if I drained our savings."

JB had better things to do than talk about his boat. He was hanging out at Raul's shop because it had a perfect view of the harbor and the adjoining parking lots. He was trying to keep track of the bad guy sent by Senator Strunk to kill him and Michael Vandorn. A photo, enlarged from the screenshot taken by Michael in the tavern where the suspected killer had met with John Melman, sat on the sill in front of him. He also had a description of the rental car. The intent of the surveillance was to monitor the movements of Senator Strunk's agent. JB and Beverly assumed Melman had blabbed about the likely locations where his targets could be found—either at Beverly's' cabin or Vandorn's boat in the harbor.

JB could clearly see the killer sitting in his rented SUV about five hundred feet away in a first-row parking space overlooking the harbor. He had known the killer would be at the harbor because Beverly had placed a tracking device on his car while he slept the previous night. So far, the guy had not moved, presumably because his target was nowhere in sight.

JB and Beverly were in a bind. They had no legal basis to incapacitate the bad guy since he had committed no crime. Consequently, they would have to lure him into attacking them so they could respond in self-defense. But that seemed like a pretty risky approach, especially since all indications were that the guy was very skilled. But the tracker gave them an advantage. JB thought the killer would eventually conclude that no one was home on the *Wonky*, give up on the harbor surveillance, and move on to the cabin. They would know if he approached the cabin and could be waiting for him. A confrontation at Beverly's cabin would be much less likely to involve collateral damage to innocent persons. All they could do was wait for the right opportunity.

At about nine o'clock, the watcher left the harbor and returned to his hotel. JB followed him back, confirmed that he entered the hotel, and then went home to Beverly's cabin. Beverly set up an alarm system on her computer that would let them know when the assassin approached the cabin. She figured they would have about ten minutes' warning—ample time to prepare. They planned to leave the cabin and hide outside, hoping that the killer would attempt to break in and give them an excuse to defend themselves.

<hr>

THE SHEARWATER ROCKED GENTLY in the waves of Seldovia Bay about fifteen miles from Homer. Charlie, Kate and Michael Vandorn lounged in the cramped pilot house, each engrossed in their own thoughts. Sea otters floated among the kelp fronds near the rocky shoreline, occasionally diving to retrieve a sea creature to eat.

"Watching the otters reminds me that I'm hungry," Kate said.

"You're always hungry," reminded Charlie.

"So, what are you thinking, Charlie?" asked Kate.

"I'm worried about JB and Beverly. I keep thinking that I should be there to help them."

"You just talked to JB on the phone ten minutes ago," Michael said. "They'll keep us informed if anything happens. I think we made the right decision to get out of Homer. JB and Beverly have both been schooled in the violent arts, whereas we have not. Even if the worst happens, we will still be alive to carry on."

"That is a very depressing way of looking at things," said Kate.

"In any event, it looks like things might finally be happening in Washington, D.C.," added Michael. "I'm extremely anxious to see how that goes."

Gloria Estevez had called earlier to inform them that an FBI team would probably be carrying out a raid later in the day.

<hr>

GEORGE SCHULER, ASSISTANT DEPUTY Secretary of the FBI, personally led the impromptu task force, mobilized the night before during the emergency meeting in the White House. Arrest warrants were issued for all the participants in the Alaska meeting at Stanley Krupp's cabin, along with Senator Strunk. Nearly all the FBI agents in the Washington D.C. area were rounded up, sworn to secrecy, and split into teams. The raids were synchronized to occur at two o'clock in the morning.

For the most part, the apprehensions occurred without incident. The participants in the conspiracy were held at a secret location, and the process of interrogation had begun. But it was no surprise to anyone that Senator Strunk had flown the coop. He had spies everywhere and had obviously been warned of his pending arrest. A search of his residence suggested that he had hastily packed and was likely on his way to another country using false travel documents.

Chapter 43

Nate Bacchus spent the night catching up on his sleep to prepare himself for a long day. After a hearty breakfast at a local café, he looked up John Melman's address on his computer, then followed his phone to Melman's hovel in the woods. Hearing someone in his drive, Melman came to the door.

"What the fuck do you want?"

"I need to know where Johann Bachman lives."

"I don't know," whined Melman.

"Bullshit," said Bacchus as he pulled out a large black handgun and forced Melman into his cabin. "Jesus, you live like a bum. Draw me a picture of the location and the setup around his place."

"Ok, maybe I have some idea," said Melman as he tore off the top of a pizza box and drew a crude map, describing the long driveway and surrounding forest.

Returning to his hotel room, Bacchus pulled up Google Earth on his computer and looked at the aerial imagery around Bachman's cabin. He thought it looked like an excellent place for a shooting. No close neighbors and lots of cover. He killed time for the rest of the day by watching television, eating and napping. At midnight, Senator Strunk's agent dressed in his nighttime work clothes—basically all black. He assembled the equipment he might need for a night raid and proceeded to Bachman's residence, taking some time to get a general idea of the setting.

When the traffic on East End Road dwindled to almost nothing, he slowly pulled into the drive.

———————

The warning alarm went off at one o'clock in the morning. Beverly and JB were already awake and dressed for the outdoors. They grabbed their prepared packs and their guns and departed out the back door and into the dense spruce. They stationed themselves a hundred feet apart so that they had views of both sides and the front door. JB donned night vision optics, making everything look an eerie green.

The late August night was dark and cool. Clouds scudded across the sky, periodically passing in front of the moon. The breeze brought with it the skunky odor of fermenting high bush cranberries, a sure sign that fall was approaching.

I think I hear a car, texted Beverly.

Got it, replied JB. *It just stopped. Sounds like he's parked a couple hundred feet down the drive. Time to be quiet.*

A couple of minutes later, a shadow appeared in the driveway and approached the cabin. The man quietly walked around the exterior, looking in the windows, then approached the back door. JB watched him pick the lock and enter the cabin. With the night vision goggles, JB could see him through the windows, going from room to room.

He's heading for the front door. I'm moving into position.

Bacchus stepped out of the cabin onto the front porch.

"Hold it right there!" yelled JB. "You're covered from two sides."

The intruder immediately dove and rolled, simultaneously firing two blind shots in the direction of JB's voice. JB fired two shots at the intruder on the ground, but the angle was poor and both shots missed. Beverly tried to move into a position where she could get a good view of the man on the ground, but the uneven terrain blocked visibility. Nevertheless, she fired two shots in his general direction. Hearing Beverly's shots, the assassin crawled behind the front porch of the cabin. Peeking over the edge of the deck, he could see Beverly partially hidden behind a small tree. He took careful aim at the small portion of Beverly's upper body that was exposed, hitting her in the left shoulder.

"Yeeow!" yelled Beverly. "I'm hit."

"Fuck!" said JB to himself as he ran obliquely toward the cabin, trying to get a better angle. More shots from the killer whizzed past him. Suddenly stopping behind one of the larger trees, he took a second to assess the situation. He could see the corner of the porch deck, but could not see the attacker. Beverly, still in the game, shot three times toward the porch, causing the assassin to reflexively move just enough so that part of his head appeared above the level of the deck. JB was ready and shot him in the side of the head. All was quiet.

JB called 911 and reported the shooting. The dispatcher said cars were already on their way because neighbors had heard the shooting. Faint sirens could be heard.

"Beverly, are you still with us?" yelled JB.

"Yeah, but I'm bleeding pretty badly. Is our intruder out of commission?"

"I think so, but I'm not sure. Can you see anything from there?"

"I can see a body on the ground."

"Ok. I'm going to move in to check."

"Be careful."

JB moved from tree to tree, then around the back of the cabin to approach the front deck from the killer's side. He saw the motionless body on the ground. The killer's gun was on the ground beside him, providing pretty strong evidence that the man was no longer a danger. He approached and felt for a pulse but found none.

———— ◆ ————

The world seemed incredibly quiet. JB found Beverly lying behind a tree with her hand on the wound. He removed his T-shirt and pressed it into the wound. The bullet had passed through the upper part of her shoulder, probably cutting a furrow through her shoulder blade, but it was pretty superficial.

"Don't go anywhere," he said to Beverly. "I need to meet the cops so they don't come in here with guns blazing."

JB walked down the driveway, only getting a hundred feet before meeting Trooper Bob. Illuminated in the headlights, he held his hands up until Bob recognized him, then quickly filled him in on the situation and Beverly's medical situation. Bob continued into the yard and directed the ambulance to Beverly's location.

JB and Bob looked at the assassin, who was definitely deceased. Of course, he had no identification. JB suggested that the guy had probably been sent by Senator Strunk to kill him.

"You're kidding me. How do you guys get into this shit? Now I'm involved in another international incident."

"Yeah, yeah. I have a feeling that the powers-that-be are going to keep this quiet. But you probably need to contact the FBI."

"Crap. That's all I need."

CHAPTER 44

CHARLIE AND KATE AWOKE on Saturday morning to the sounds of seabirds chattering around the *Shearwater*. The day was bright and clear, and the view from their anchorage in Seldovia Bay was spectacular. The scenic town of Seldovia lay to the east, nestled at the base of low mountains accented by stripes of snow alternating with stripes of dark green grass on the hillsides high above the town. Looking west across Cook Inlet, Augustine Volcano loomed above the sea, topped by a disk-shaped lenticular cloud. Charlie was sitting on the edge of the bed, pulling on his sweats at about seven o'clock when his phone rang.

"You're up pretty early, JB," said Charlie as he woke Kate and turned the phone on speaker.

"We've had a pretty eventful night. Senator Strunk's agent is dead, and Beverly's in the hospital with a bullet through the shoulder."

"Oh, crap," Kate said as she suddenly became wide awake.

"Hang on," replied Charlie as he climbed the companionway from the master suite and entered the pilot house. "Let me wake up Michael, and you can tell us the whole story."

"What's Beverly's exact condition?" asked Kate.

"She's doing fine. The bullet grazed the top of her shoulder and took out a chunk of collarbone. It's painful, but she's not in any danger. I'm in her hospital room, and she's actually quite happy right now, flying on pain pills."

"G'morning, everybody," slurred Beverly.

"So, exactly how did Strunk's guy get dead?" asked Kate.

"I shot him," replied JB. "After he shot Beverly."

"Holy shit."

JB related the entire chain of events that had transpired the previous night, followed by a flurry of questions from the Homer refugees.

"Is this whole nightmare finally over?" asked Kate.

"Maybe," said Beverly. "Have you guys heard from Gloria Estevez? Do we have any idea what's going on in Washington?"

"I'm going to call her as soon as I've had my coffee," said Michael as he put on his pants.

"You sound pretty good, Beverly," Kate said with tears in her eyes. "Oh, crap! Now I'm blubbering."

"I'm really Ok. I'll see you guys soon."

———◆———

COINCIDENTALLY, MICHAEL'S BURNER PHONE rang just as he finished his second cup of coffee.

"Good morning, Gloria. I hope you have good news. You're on speaker with Charlie and Kate."

"It's mostly good. Last night, the FBI coordinated a raid on all the persons on the infamous cabin tape. They are all currently being detained, but I suspect most of them will be out on bail pretty soon. In any event, it's all out of your hands for the time being."

"Wow, that's great. What's the not-so-good news?"

"Senator Strunk was nowhere to be found. Presumably, he got wind of the raid somehow. He is probably out of the country."

"That's too bad. He's the one guy we have enough evidence on to keep in jail."

"On the other hand, my analyst is trying to track his whereabouts. It may take a while, since I'm sure he's using a different identity. But we'll find him. His being out of the country may actually be an advantage."

"I'll pretend I didn't hear that. We've got some good news for you, too. Last night, JB and Beverly had a shootout with Strunk's assassin at their cabin. He was killed. Unfortunately, Beverly got shot in the shoulder, but she's going to be fine."

"Wow. That's fuckin' great. Not for Beverly, of course. Maybe you guys can breathe easier. At least until y'all have to come to D.C. to testify in the trials for our merry band of traitors."

"I suppose that's a possibility, but a lot of those guys will likely settle without a trial."

"I'm sure you'll be getting some calls from your Justice Department colleagues very soon. Anyway, you guys enjoy some well-deserved relaxation, and thanks for everything you've done. I have to go. As you can imagine, the shit is hitting the fan here, and my phone is ringing off the hook."

Gloria signed off, and Michael called JB and Beverly with the news. It looked like things really were going to cool down. Charlie fired up the big engine on the *Shearwater*, weighed anchor, and headed for home.

Chapter 45

*S*MALL BRANCHES WHIPPED HER *in the face, and sharp spruce needles scratched her arms as she ran through the dense forest. She heard the crashing footsteps of the man chasing her, seeming to get closer and closer as she stumbled over the uneven forest floor. She caught her foot on a tree root and fell forward onto her face. Twisting her body and looking back, she saw the man in the black balaclava approach and aim his gun . . .*

"Ahh," moaned Beverly as she awoke, her eyes suddenly popping open. She realized that she was surrounded by bodies. Every square inch of her small hospital room was occupied. All the Mooseketeers, plus Michael Vandorn and the Super Trooper, were present. JB sat in a chair by the hospital bed holding her hand.

"Are we having a party?" asked Beverly, still groggy from the anesthesia required while the doctors repaired her shoulder.

"That must have been quite a dream," said Charlie. "Are you back in the land of the living?"

"I think so. More or less."

"The doctors say your shoulder will be fine, but it is going to hurt for a while until the bone heals," said JB. "I suppose I'm going to have to put up with your whining."

"You got that right," quipped Beverly. "And you may have to do the cooking for a while."

"Thank God for pizza delivery," said JB.

The adventures of the night before were recounted once again, with the amount of drama increasing with each retelling. Finally, they had exhausted all of the news.

"So, Bob, what's going to happen now with the investigation of the shooting?" asked Beverly, now wide awake.

"I suggest you and JB come into the office as soon as you're discharged and make detailed statements of what transpired. I also suggest you omit the parts about the tracker on the assassin's vehicle and lying in wait for the bad guy. Maybe just say you heard him approach the front door, so you went out the back. Tell the truth about how the shootout went down. We've done a pretty thorough examination of the area around your cabin—bullet casings, blood, and so forth—and everything seems consistent with your account. Alaska has liberal laws regarding defense of property, so I don't see anybody having severe heartburn. Your weapons are legal, so that's not an issue. The fact that Beverly was shot first should eliminate any suspicion of extra-legal activity."

"Thanks, Bob," said JB. "Has the body been identified?"

"His ID papers said his name was Nate Bacchus. But his fingerprints came back under the name Fred Halberstam. He is a former Marine and has recently been employed by a lobbying firm called Gentle Persuasion."

"Holy cow," said Michael. "That's Stanley Krupp's company. Yet another connection between Project Nemesis, Stanley Krupp, and Senator Strunk. I'll tell Gloria to investigate the company and, hopefully, shut it down. It looks like things are finally getting wrapped up."

"So, Michael, what are you going to do now?" asked Kate.

"I think I'm going to spend a few days getting experience on my brother's boat, and then take a leisurely trip back down to the Pacific Northwest. I suppose I'll go back to work as a Prosecutor if they'll let me back. Hopefully, there won't be political backlash because of my activities up here."

———◆———

On a beautiful early fall day Charlie, Kate, JB, and Beverly sat on the small front porch of Kate's long-neglected log cabin in the woods. Buster the cat, sphinxlike, staked out the woodpile, waiting for the appearance of a yummy red-backed vole. Mosquitoes and flies buzzed around the quartet in an annoying fashion, deflected by DEET. The musty-sweet smells of fall emanated from the adjacent bog and spruce forest. Busy red squirrels scritched in the trees looking for spruce cones to store for the winter. Cones rained from the trees as the small mammals dropped them to the ground and cached them for the harder times to come.

"Michael left this morning for his journey to the Pacific Northwest," said Charlie as he sipped his hot cocoa. "I hope all goes well. He was a fast learner and shouldn't have any trouble."

"He's a pretty great guy," added Kate. "We're going to miss him."

"Yeah, what are we going to do without a crisis?" said JB.

"I, for one, am looking forward to a peaceful fall," said Beverly between bug swats with her one good arm. "Have we heard anything from the Homeland Security Secretary?"

"I got a text yesterday which said that the cases against the conspirators are proceeding, albeit slowly as usual," Charlie said. "Except for the case against Stanley Krupp, which was more straightforward. He's scheduled to go on trial in a couple of weeks."

"Any word about Senator Strunk?" asked Beverly.

"Gloria was a little cagey when I asked her about that," said Charlie. "I have a feeling that we will never know what happens to the senator."

"Well, here's to peace and quiet," said Kate as all clinked cocoa cups

Epilogue

Five weeks later.
Little Cayman Chronicle, Oct. 3:
Body Found in East End Villa

Two days ago, the body of an elderly man was found by a maintenance person in a secluded seaside villa at the east end of Little Cayman Island. According to authorities, the man had been shot, and the incident is being treated as a homicide. His passport was found on site and identified him as seventy-three-year-old Stuart Fox of Newport, Virginia. Nearby residents said the man was reclusive and little was known about him. He had arrived a month earlier and quietly taken up residence in the upscale estate. Julie Laplante, owner of a local convenience store, indicated that the man occasionally stopped in for beer and whiskey. She said the man spoke English with an American southern accent and was often rude and impolite.

Authorities researching the man's identity were mystified by the general lack of information available through normal channels and suspect that the passport was forged. If anyone has information about this person, please contact the Little Cayman Police.

Acknowledgements

Numerous people and organizations helped to bring "Project Nemesis" to the finish line. I would like to thank Ethan Zimmerman for his editing prowess—finding all the missing commas was no small task. My granddaughter, Hannah Morsell, created the cover illustration. Melissa Coffman of Book House Publishing crafted the cover layout and text format. The Publishing Department of Village Books in Bellingham, Washington coordinated the effort through their excellent self-publishing program.

Last, but not least, I would like to thank the members of the Thursday afternoon writers critique group in Hamilton, Montana for their insights and suggestions.